R0085169407

07/2017

D0984313

The moment Nikos's mouth touched hers, Georgia jolted, as if she'd stumbled into a live wire. Sensation rushed through her in electric waves, making her shudder.

Nikos deepened the kiss, his lips parting hers, and she shuddered again at the pleasure of his tongue stroking the inside of her sensitive lower lip and then finding her upper lip.

It had been ages since she'd kissed anyone. She couldn't even remember her last kiss.

Nikos was in total control, drawing her close, his hard body pressed to the length of her as lips and tongue made her melt. She felt hot and explosive, her blood humming in her veins. She shuddered as his hand moved beneath her long hair to cup her nape and then moved down her neck, stirring every nerve-ending in her skin.

This was unlike any kiss she'd ever known.

This was shockingly electric.

Chemistry.

She fled. It was that or collapse in a puddle on the kitchen floor.

In her room, she locked the door and leaned against it, legs still shaking.

What had just happened?

She'd never felt anything so consuming…pleasure and hunger and something else…something so intense that it continued to ripple through her in hot, dizzying waves.

Desire. Lust. Need.

Georgia exhaled slowly, trying to get control, needing to clear her head, and yet all she could feel was the pressure of Nikos's body against hers and the feel of his mouth…as well as his taste.

He'd tasted like heat and honey and liquorice. She'd never tasted anything like it. And, God help her, she wanted more.

New York Times and *USA TODAY* bestselling author **Jane Porter** has written forty romances and eleven women's fiction novels since her first sale to Mills & Boon Modern Romance in 2000. A five-time RITA® Award finalist, Jane is known for her passionate, emotional and sensual novels, and she loves nothing more than alpha heroes, exotic locations and happy-ever-afters. Today Jane lives in sunny San Clemente, California, with her surfer husband and three sons. Visit www.janeporter.com.

Books by Jane Porter

Mills & Boon Modern Romance

The Disgraced Copelands

A Royal Scandal

The Desert Kings

Greek Tycoons

Ruthless

Desert Brides

Visit the Author Profile page at millsandboon.co.uk for more titles.

BOUGHT TO
CARRY HIS HEIR

BY
JANE PORTER

First Published in Great Britain 2016
By Mills & Boon, an imprint of HarperCollins*Publishers*
1 London Bridge Street, London, SE1 9GF

© 2016 Jane Porter

ISBN: 978-0-263-06806-1

Printed and bound in Great Britain
by CPI Antony Rowe, Chippenham, Wiltshire

BOUGHT TO
CARRY HIS HEIR

For Megan, Maisey and Carol—
three gorgeous girls I adore.
Thank you for the love and encouragement when I needed it!

CHAPTER ONE

IT WAS A cold February afternoon in Atlanta, but the law office of Lyles, Laurent & Abraham at One Atlantic Center on West Peachtree Street was even more frigid.

The prominent Atlanta attorney James Laurent fiddled with his glasses, his expression withering. "You signed the contracts, Miss Nielsen. They are absolutely binding in every country—"

"I have no problem with the contract," Georgia interrupted, more annoyed than cowed by the attorney's icy contempt, because she was absolutely committed to carrying the baby only to relinquish him. That was the job of a surrogate, and she took the job seriously. "The baby is his. But there is nothing in the contract that stipulates where I am to give birth, nor was anything ever communicated to me in advance about giving birth overseas. I wouldn't have agreed to serve as Mr. Panos's surrogate if that had been the case."

"Miss Nielsen, Greece is not a third world country. You will receive excellent medical care in Athens before, during and after delivery."

She gave him a long look, hands relaxed on the arms of the leather chair, fighting to keep her temper in check. "I'm a med student at Emory. I'm not worried about my medical care. But I am disturbed by your condescension. If a mistake was made, it was your client's...or yours. You were, after all, the one who drew up the papers for the surrogacy. You know what the agreement covered. And it didn't cover me getting on a plane and flying five thousand six hundred and sixty-six miles to give birth."

"It's a citizenship issue, Miss Nielsen. The baby must be born in Greece."

Georgia Nielsen glanced past the attorney to the huge map that had been framed and hung on the wall of Mr. Laurent's office. It was an old map, a collector's item, and from the boundaries and labels, she'd guess it was from the late nineteenth century, the 1880s or maybe 1890s, with Africa divided by European colonial claims. But even old and yellowed, Greece was identifiable...right where it had been for thousands of years, giving birth to Western civilization.

And right where she was expected to give birth.

If Georgia were in a better mood, she might find it ironic. She might even be amused. But she wasn't in a good mood. She was furious and frustrated. From the start, she'd taken care of herself, paid close attention to proper health and the well-being of the baby. Her job as a surrogate was to bear a healthy baby, and she was doing her part. Eating right, sleeping as much as possible, getting lots of exercise and keeping stress to a minimum—not always easy when in medical school, but she had her priorities right. But going to Greece? And going soon? That was *not* on her agenda.

"The travel arrangements are being finalized as we speak," Mr. Laurent added. "Mr. Panos will send his personal jet for you. As you can imagine, the jet is state-of-the-art and quite luxurious. You'll have staff and a good rest, and before you know it, you'll be there—"

"I haven't even reached the third trimester. Seems to me that making travel plans now is incredibly premature."

"Mr. Panos would prefer not to place undue stress on you or the baby. Specialists do not recommend international travel in the third trimester."

"Yes, for high-risk pregnancies, but this isn't one."

"It is IVF."

"There have been no complications."

"And my client prefers to keep it that way."

Georgia bit her tongue to keep from saying something she might regret. She understood that Nikos Panos's concern was for the baby, his son. She understood, too, that her wants and needs did not factor in. She was a vessel…a womb…nothing more. As it should be until the very end, when she delivered a healthy baby and saw him placed in the arms of his protective father. That was when her job would be done. Then, and only then.

But that didn't mean she wanted to leave Atlanta or the world she knew. Going halfway around the world would be stressful. Leaving her support systems would be challenging, especially as she neared the end of the pregnancy. This was a job, a way to provide for her sister, but she wasn't totally naive. It was hard not to have any feelings for the life inside her, and those emotions were becoming stronger. Hormones were already shifting. She could only imagine how ambivalent she'd feel in another three and a half months.

But motherhood wasn't her future. Her future was medicine, and her course was set.

For a long moment there was just silence in the office.

Mr. Laurent pressed his fingers together, creating a tense steeple. "What will it take to get you on that plane this Friday?"

Ridiculous. There was no way she could go so soon. "I have school. I have studies."

"You have just finished the preclinical block. You are studying for the medical licensing exam, and you can study just as well in Greece as in Georgia."

"I'm not going to leave my sister for three and a half months."

"She's twenty-one and lives in North Carolina."

"Yes, she's a senior at Duke University, but she's financially and emotionally dependent on me. I am her only living relative." Georgia met his gaze and held it. "I am all she has left."

"And the child you carry?"

"Isn't mine." Her lips firmed. "Your client paid for the egg and the surrogacy, so if Mr. Panos wants to be present for the birth of his son, he can come to Atlanta. Otherwise, the baby's nurse will take the infant to him. As agreed."

"Mr. Panos is not able to fly."

Georgia lifted her chin, air bottled inside her lungs. She was not going to engage. She refused to be drawn into this. A contract was a contract. "That is not my concern. Your client is not my concern. Once I give birth, the infant is not my concern. I have been paid not to care, and, Mr. Laurent, I intend to keep my end of the bargain."

The attorney closed his eyes and rubbed at an invisible spot between his bushy gray eyebrows, bumping his glasses from his nose. For a moment the only sound in the room was the antique grandfather clock tick-ticking against the wall.

Mr. Laurent opened his eyes, fixed his gaze on her. "How much will it cost to get you on the plane on Friday? And before you say I'm not listening, I know everyone has a price. You do, too. It's why you agreed to donate the egg and carry the fertilized embryo. You were satisfied with the compensation. So, let's not bicker over the terms. Tell me what you need to get on that plane, and I will see that the money is wired into your account first thing in the morning."

Georgia stared at the older man, her serene expression hiding her anxiety, as well as her frustration. Yes, money was tight, but she didn't want more money. She just wanted to finish what she'd started. It had been a mistake to do this. She thought she'd manage as a surrogate, but lately she was finding it increasingly difficult to keep her emotions in check. But it was too late to back out now. There was no changing her mind, either. The contracts were binding. The child wasn't hers. And, yes, she carried him, and each little flutter kick made her heart ache, but the baby was Nikos Panos's, and she couldn't forget it.

Which meant she had to move forward. It was her only option. And the moment she delivered, the moment the baby was whisked away, she'd black this year from her memory. Georgia never wanted to think about any of this again. It was the only way to survive something so challenging. Fortunately, she had practice in surviving challenging situations. Grief was a good teacher.

"Name it," Mr. Laurent said quietly.

"It's not about the money—"

"But it will pay bills, so pay your bills. Provide for your sister. I understand she, too, wants to attend medical school. Take advantage of the offer so you never have to do something like this again."

That last bit hit home. Her gaze locked with his, and her short, filed nails curled into her palms.

Mr. Laurent was right. She could never do something like this again. It was breaking her heart. But she'd survived worse. And it wasn't as if she was abandoning a child to a monster. Nikos Panos wanted this baby desperately.

Drawing a short, sharp breath, Georgia named an outrageous figure, a sum that would cover Savannah's medical school and living expenses, plus some. Georgia made the sum deliberately high, intending to shock the old lawyer.

But Mr. Laurent didn't blink. Instead he scribbled something down on a printed sheet of paper. "The addendum," he said, pushing the paper across the desk toward her. "Sign here, and date there."

She swallowed, shocked he'd so readily agreed to her "outrageous" demand. He must have been prepared for her to ask for even more. She probably could have asked for millions and he would have said yes. Stupid pride. Why couldn't she be a proper mercenary?

"You're agreeing to leave Friday," Mr. Laurent said as she reached for the page. "You will spend the last trimester of your pregnancy in Greece, at Nikos Panos's villa on Kamari, which is a short flight from Athens. After delivery, once you have been cleared to travel, my client will send you back to Atlanta, either on his private jet or first class on the airline of your choice. Any questions?"

"The money? It will be wired into my account first thing tomorrow?"

He handed her a pen. "It will be there by nine a.m." He smiled as she signed.

"I'm so glad we were able to come to terms."

Georgia stood, heartsick but too far in to see a way out. "As you said, everyone has a price. Goodbye, Mr. Laurent."

"Enjoy your time in Greece, Miss Nielsen."

CHAPTER TWO

It was a long trip from Atlanta. Nearly thirteen hours, which meant that Georgia had plenty of time to sleep, study and even watch a movie or two when she was too tired to read one more sample question from the test.

The movies helped occupy her mind. She didn't want to think. If she wasn't going to sleep, she needed entertainment and diversion to keep from replaying her goodbye with Savannah, who'd driven down from Duke to see her off.

Or more accurately, who'd driven down to beg Georgia not to go.

Savannah had been beside herself, alternating between tears and anger, asking repeatedly what Georgia knew about this Greek tycoon in the first place.

What do you even know about him? And who cares if he's a billionaire? He could be dangerous, seriously deranged, and who will be able to help you when you're on his island in the middle of nowhere?

Savannah had never been the practical one, but in this instance, she was right.

Georgia had researched Nikos Panos—and, yes, he was a Greek billionaire, and he'd turned his family's struggling company around with shrewd investments, and he'd done it at a young age, taking over the helm of the company while in his midtwenties—but she didn't have any references on him. Nothing on his morals or his character. She just had the attorney and the payments for services rendered.

She started to rub her tummy. Her bump was becoming increasingly pronounced. Her skin was sensitive, and warm, and even when she didn't want to think about the pregnancy, or the surrogacy, she was aware of the life inside her.

And not just a life, but a boy. There were no boys in her family. Just girls. Three sisters. Georgia couldn't even imagine what it'd be like to raise a little boy.

But she wouldn't go there. She never let herself go there. She wasn't going to let herself become invested.

But as the jet made its final descent into what looked like an endless sea of blue, the baby did a flutter kick as if recognizing that he was almost home. Georgia held her breath, fighting panic.

She could do this. She would do this.

The baby wasn't hers.

She wasn't attached.

She'd been paid not to care.

She wouldn't care.

But those fierce admonishments did little to ease the wave of grief and regret washing through her heart.

"Just three and a half months," she whispered. Three and a half months and she'd be free of this horrific thing she'd agreed to do.

Three and a half months, Nikos Panos told himself, standing at the far end of the landing strip, narrowed gaze fixed on the white Dassault Falcon jet. It had been a rough landing owing to the windy day, which wasn't unusual for this time of year in the Cyclades. But the jet was safely parked and the door was open, revealing twenty-four-year-old Georgia Nielsen.

From where he stood, she appeared very slender and very blonde in a soft-knit apricot tunic, dark gray tights and high-heel boots that covered her knees. He frowned at the height of the heels on her boots, baffled as to why a pregnant woman would wear boots with heels four inches high. Her boots were a problem, and so was her dress.

Her tunic's knit hem hit just above midthigh, revealing a lot of leg.

Nikos knew from her profile that Georgia Nielsen would be pretty, but he hadn't expected *this*.

Standing at the top of the stairs with the blustery wind grabbing at her hair and the sun haloing the bright golden mass, she looked so much like Elsa that it made his chest tighten and ache.

He'd wanted a surrogate that looked like Elsa.

But he didn't want Elsa.

In that moment, he wondered if he'd made a terrible mistake. He had to be more than a little bit mad to search the world for a woman that looked like his late wife, and certifiably insane to bring that doppelgänger here, to Kamari.

The American surrogate must have spotted him because she suddenly straightened, and, lifting a hand to her hair, held the billowing golden mane back from her face as she came down the jet's stairs quickly. It wasn't quite a run, but definitely with speed, and purpose.

Not Elsa, he grimly corrected, moving forward to meet her.

His Elsa had been quiet and gentle, even a bit timid, while this leggy blonde crossed the tarmac as if she owned it. He met her halfway, determined to slow her down. "Careful," he ground out.

Georgia lifted her head and looked at him, brows pulling. "Of what?" she countered, a hint of irritation in her voice.

From afar she was striking. Close, she was astonishingly pretty. Even prettier than Elsa, maybe, if such a thing was possible.

And for the second time he thought this was a critical error, bringing her here, now, when there was so much time left before the baby's birth. Not because he was in danger of falling in love with his late wife's ghost, but because his relationship with Elsa had never been easy, and her sense-less death had filled him with guilt. He hoped the baby would ease some of the guilt. He hoped that becoming a father would force him to move forward and live. And feel.

Elsa wasn't the only ghost in his life. He'd become one, too.

"You could trip and fall," he said shortly, his deep voice rough even to his own ears. He didn't speak much on Kamari. Not even to his staff. They knew their duties, and they did them without unnecessary conversation.

One of her winged eyebrows arched higher. She gave him a long, assessing look, sizing him up—inspecting, cataloging, making a dozen mental notes. "I wouldn't do that," she said after a moment. "I have excellent balance. I would have loved to be a gymnast, but I grew too tall." She extended her hand to him. "But I appreciate your con-cern, Mr. Panos."

He looked down at her hand for what would probably be considered too long to be polite. He'd never been overly concerned about manners and niceties before the fire, and now he simply didn't care at all. He didn't care about any-thing. That was the problem. But the Panoses couldn't die out with him. Not just because the company needed an heir; he was the last Panos. It wasn't right that he al-lowed his mistakes to end hundreds of years of a family lineage. Surely his family shouldn't pay for who he was... what he'd done...

The baby would hopefully change that. The child would be the future. God knew he needed a future.

Taking her hand, his fingers engulfed hers, his grip firm, her skin warm against his. "Nikos," he corrected.

Then he lifted his head and turned his jaw from her to give her a good look at the right side of his face, letting her see who he was now. What he was now.

A monster.

The Beast of Kamari.

He turned his head back the other way and met her gaze.

She looked straight back at him without a flicker of horror or fear. Nor did she reveal surprise. Instead her blue eyes, with their specks of gray and bits of silver, were wide and clear. He found it intriguing that she didn't appear discomfited by the burns on his temple and cheek.

"Georgia," she replied, giving his hand an equally firm shake.

Like the proverbial Georgia peach, he thought, releasing her hand. Her name suited her. Too well.

Despite the long hours flying, despite the pregnancy—or maybe because of it—she looked fresh, ripe, glowing with health and vitality.

Nikos, who hadn't wanted anything or anyone for nearly five years, felt the stirring of curiosity, and the dull ache of desire. He hadn't felt anything in so long that the stirring of his body was as surprising as the questions forming in his mind.

Was the attraction because she resembled Elsa, or was he intrigued because she seemed fearless when confronted by his scars?

Touching her hand, feeling her warmth, made something within him uncoil and reach out to her, wondering just who she was, wondering what she looked like naked, wondering what she would taste like if he put his mouth to her skin—

And just like that, after years of feeling nothing, and being nothing, and living as if numb or dead, he hardened, his body responding to her despite whatever else was happening in his head.

And yet this was what couldn't happen. And this was why he lived on Kamari, away from people. It wasn't to protect himself, but to protect others.

Nikos ruthlessly clamped down on the surge of desire, smashing it by reminding himself of what he'd done to Elsa, and what Elsa's death had done to him.

But she wasn't Elsa, wasn't his wife. And even though she wasn't a wife, he still wouldn't take chances. She carried his son. Her health and well-being were essential for his son's health and well-being. And so he'd take excellent care of the surrogate, but only because she was the surrogate. She was nothing to him beyond that. Just help…a hired womb…that was all.

All, he repeated, looking past her to his flight crew. He gestured, indicating that her luggage should be placed in the back of the restored 1961 military Land Rover. It was the best vehicle for Kamari's rugged terrain, handling the steep twisting roads with ease. It was also his preferred vehicle since he could drive in summer without the soft top. In winter he kept the soft top up, but there were no windows. No glass to trap him.

He started for the vehicle, and then remembered the American's ridiculous footwear. "Those shoes are not appropriate for Kamari," he said curtly.

She gave him another long look and then shrugged. "I'll keep that in mind," she said before setting off, heading toward the passenger side of his green Land Rover with her careless, leggy, athletic grace, the wind catching at her bright hair, making it shimmer and dance.

Definitely not Elsa, he thought.

Nothing about Elsa shimmered and danced. But she had once, hadn't she? She'd been happy once…before she'd married him. Before she'd come to regret everything about her life with him…

Nikos smashed his hand into a tight fist, squeezing hard, fighting the past that haunted him always. He prayed the baby would mean new life…not just for the child but for him, too. He prayed that if he were a good father, he'd find peace. Redemption.

Or was it too late for that?

He forced his attention to Georgia. A footstool had been placed on the ground for her, making it easier for her to enter the lifted four-wheel drive vehicle, but she seemed amused by the stool, her full lips quirking as she stepped onto it and swung easily into the passenger seat.

He didn't understand her smile. He didn't understand such brazen confidence, either. She seemed to be throwing down the gauntlet. Challenging him.

He wasn't sure he liked it. She'd only just arrived.

Fortunately he had his temper well in check. His pulse had quickened, but he was still in control. Once upon a time his temper had been legendary. But it was better now that he was older. He'd matured, thank God. He'd never really lost his temper with Elsa, but she'd been nervous around him. Skittish.

He shook his head, chasing away the memories. He didn't want to think of Elsa now. Didn't want to be haunted by the past any longer. It was why he'd hired the donor and surrogate. He was trying to move forward, trying to create a future where there hadn't been one in far too long.

Climbing behind the steering wheel, he glanced at Georgia. She was fastening her seat belt and pale, gleaming hair spilled over her shoulders and down her back like a golden waterfall. Beautiful hair. Longer than Elsa's had ever been.

Nikos felt a lance of appreciation, and then clamped down on the sensation, more than a little bit baffled by his attraction. He didn't want to find Georgia Nielsen attractive. Didn't want to find anything about her attractive. She was here as a surrogate...

A vessel.

A womb.

But his body had a mind of its own, and the heavy ache

in his groin grew, his body tight with a testosterone-fueled tension that made him ruthless and restless. A tiger on the prowl. A beast out of the cage.

He didn't like feeling this way. He didn't like anything— or anyone—that tested him, challenging him, reminding him of his dark edges. He hadn't known until he married Elsa that he had such a frightening personality. He hadn't known until Elsa began hiding from him that he was such a beast…a monster…

Thirio.

Teras.

If he'd known who he was before he married, he wouldn't have married. If he'd known he would destroy his beautiful wife with his temper, he would have remained a bachelor.

And yet he'd wanted children. He'd very much wanted to create a family. To have people of his own…

From the corner of his eye he saw Georgia cross one leg over the other, drawing his attention to her legs. The tunic hit high on her thigh and the boots stopped at her knee and her legs, in the gray tights, were slim and shapely.

"We're about fifteen minutes from the house," he said roughly, starting the engine, battling his thoughts, battling the desire that made him feel as if he had gasoline in his veins instead of blood.

"And town?" she asked, adjusting the belt across her lap.

His gaze followed, focusing on her waist. For the first time, he could see the gentle swell of her belly. She was most definitely pregnant. The cut of the cashmere tunic had just hidden the bump earlier.

The bump jolted him. *His* child. *His* son.

For a split second he couldn't breathe. It was suddenly real. The life he'd made…his seed…her egg…

"Do you want to touch him?" she asked quietly.

He looked up into her face. Her cheeks were pale, and

yet her gaze was direct, steady. "He's moving around," she added, lips curving faintly. "I think he's saying hello."

Nikos dropped his gaze to her hands resting at her side, and then back to the gentle curve of her belly.

"Isn't it too soon for me to feel him moving?" he asked.

"It might have been a week or two ago, but not anymore."

He stared at her bump for another moment, conflicted. He wanted to feel his son kick, but he couldn't bring himself to touch her, not wanting to feel the tautness of her belly or the warmth of her skin. She wasn't supposed to matter in any way, and yet suddenly she wasn't this vessel, this hired womb, but a stunning young woman carrying his son.

"Not right now," he said, fingers curling around the stick shift, changing gears, driving forward. His gut was hard, tight. Air ached in his lungs. What had he done bringing this woman to him? How could he have thought this would be a good idea? "But it is good to know that he's moving and seems healthy."

"He's very healthy. I trust you've been getting the reports and sonograms from my checkups?"

"Yes." But he didn't want to talk about the baby. He didn't want to talk at all. She was here now so she didn't have to fly late in the third trimester, but he hadn't brought her to Kamari to create a friendship. There would be no relationship between them. He needed her to be safe, but beyond that he wanted nothing more to do with her, and the sooner she understood that, the better.

"And town?" she repeated, catching a fistful of billowing golden hair.

He shifted gears as he accelerated. "There's no town. It's a private island."

She was looking at him now. "Yours?"

"Mine," he agreed.

"And the house? What's that like?"

"It's close to the water, which is nice in summer."

"But not as nice in winter?"

He shot her a swift glance. "It's an old house. Simple. But it suits me."

Her hand shifted on her mass of hair. "Mr. Laurent referred to it as a villa." She shot him another curious look. "Was he wrong?"

"In Greece, a villa is usually one's country house. So, no, he wasn't wrong, but I myself do not use that word. This is where I live now. It's my home."

She opened her mouth to ask another question but he cut her short, his tone flat and flinty even to his own ears. "I am not much of a conversationalist, Georgia."

If Georgia hadn't been quite so queasy, she might have laughed. Was that his way of telling her to stop asking questions?

She shot him a swift glance, taking in his hard carved features and the black slash of eyebrows above dark eyes.

Just looking at him made her feel jittery, putting an odd whoosh in her middle, almost as if she were back on the plane and coming in for that rocky landing all over again.

He wasn't what she'd expected. She'd imagined a solid, comfortably built tycoon in his early to midthirties, but there was nothing comfortable about Nikos Panos. He was tall with broad shoulders and long limbs. He had thick, glossy black hair, piercing eyes and beautiful features... at least on one half of his face. The other side was scarred around the temple and cheekbone. The scars were significant but not grotesque, but then she understood what they were—burns—and she could only imagine how painful the healing process must have been.

If one could look past the scars, he was the stuff of little girls' fairy tales and teenage fantasies.

Correction, if you could look past the scars and brusque manner.

I am not much of a conversationalist, Georgia.

What did that even mean? Was there no one she would be able to talk to during her stay here?

Mr. Laurent had told her there was no Mrs. Panos. Mr. Laurent had said his client would be raising the child as a single father. Was this where the child would be raised?

On this arid volcanic island, in the middle of this sea?

"Where will you live?" she asked abruptly. "Once the baby is born?"

His black eyebrows flattened. "Here. This is my home."

Georgia held her breath and stared out at the narrow road that clung to the side of the mountain. The road was single lane, barely paved, and it snaked down and around the hillside. She wished there was a guardrail.

She wished she was back in Atlanta.

She wished she'd never agreed to any of this.

Georgia fought her anxiety and practiced breathing—a slow, measured inhale, followed by an even slower exhale.

Why was she doing this? Why was she here?

The money.

Her chest ached with bottled air. She was doing it for the money.

Sometimes focusing on the two huge sums that had been wired to her bank account gave her perspective when her hormones and emotions threatened to overwhelm her, but it wasn't working now.

Maybe it was the long flight or jet lag or just the relentless nausea, but Georgia's stomach heaved once, and then again. "Please pull over," she begged, grabbing the car's door handle. "I'm going to be sick."

CHAPTER THREE

IN HER ROOM at the villa, Georgia slept for hours, sleeping away the remainder of the day.

She dreamed of Savannah, of her goodbye with Savannah yesterday, her younger sister's emotional cry playing out in her dream.

What do you even know about him?

He could be dangerous...seriously deranged...

Who will be able to help you when you're on his island in the middle of nowhere?

The dream was broken by the dull, but insistent, pounding on her bedroom door.

Georgia heard it but didn't want to wake, and for a moment she lay in the strange bed, heart racing, pulse pounding, late-afternoon sunlight slanting through wooden blinds, as she tried to cling to the last of the dream, missing Savannah already.

But the knocking on her door wouldn't stop.

Georgia dragged herself into a sitting position and was just about to rise when her door crashed open and Nikos came charging into her room.

"What on earth are you doing?" she cried, rising.

"Why didn't you answer the damn door?"

"I was asleep!"

"We've been trying to rouse you for the past hour." He stalked toward the bed, his dark eyes glittering. "I thought you were dead."

She pulled on the hem of her cotton pajama top, trying to hide the skin gaping beneath. She was just starting to need maternity clothes. She hadn't bought any maternity wear until recently, not wanting to spend money until absolutely necessary. "Not dead, as you can see."

"You gave me quite a scare," he gritted out.

She was still trembling with shock. She lifted a hand to show him how badly her hand shook. "How do you think I feel? You broke my door—"

"It can be fixed."

"But who does that? I thought that was just cops in movies."

"I'll have someone repair it when you come upstairs for lunch."

She wanted an apology, but it seemed she wasn't going to get it. He really didn't think he'd done anything wrong. Georgia glanced to the shuttered window with the late-afternoon sunlight stabbing through the gaps and cracks in the wood, trying to calm down and regain her composure. "I would think it's dinnertime, not lunch."

"We don't eat dinner until ten or later, so we're having a late lunch for you now. Dress and come upstairs—"

"Can you not send something to the room?" she interrupted, irritated all over again by his curtness. He lacked manners and the basic social graces. "After the long flight I would prefer to stay in my pajamas and just read a bit—"

"Head straight up the stairs to the third floor, we're on the second floor now, and then through the living room to the doors to the terrace," he concluded as if she'd never spoken.

She frowned, increasingly annoyed. "Mr. Laurent led me to believe that I would be able to have my own space and as much privacy as I desired."

"You have your own space. Three rooms, all for you. But once a day we will meet and visit and have a meal together, and we might as well begin tonight as it will help establish a routine."

"I don't see why we need to meet daily. We have nothing to say to each other."

"That is correct, and I am in complete agreement. You and I have nothing to say to each other, but I have plenty to say to my son, and since he is inside of you, you are required to be present, as well."

She clamped her jaw tight to hold back the caustic comment that was tingling on the tip of her tongue, and then she couldn't. "I am sorry you have to endure my dreadful company for the next three months, then."

"We both are making sacrifices," he answered. "Fortunately, you are being compensated for yours." He nodded at her and turned to leave.

"I would like to shower first."

"Fine."

She had to hold back another caustic comment. "And you'll have someone repair the door while I'm upstairs?"

"I already said that."

Leaving Georgia's room, Nikos summoned Adras, the older man who oversaw the running of the villa, and told him that his guest's bedroom door needed to be repaired. And then Nikos went up to the shaded, whitewashed terrace to wait for Georgia.

The sun had shifted, deepening the colors of the sky and sea. The terrace was protected from the worst of the wind, with the most protection closest to the house. Nikos stood at the wall, looking out over the sea, and the wind caught at his shirt and hair. His hair was perhaps too long, but it helped hide the scars on his temple and cheekbone.

It was easy to ignore the breeze as he was anticipating Georgia's appearance. It was strange to have her in the house. He wasn't used to having visitors. Kamari was his own rock, 323 acres in the northwestern Cyclades in the Aegean Sea. Amorgós was the closest island to Kamari, with a hospital, ferry, shops and monastery, but Nikos hadn't been to Amorgós in years. There was no point. There was nothing good on Amorgós...not for him.

Instead everything he needed was flown in from the mainland, and if he wanted company, he'd fly to Athens. Not that he ever wanted company. It'd been months and months since he'd left his rock. He had a home in Athens, along with his corporate headquarters. He had another place on Santorini, but that was the old family estate, a former winery that had once been his favorite place in the world and now the source of his nightmares.

Nikos had lived alone so long that he couldn't imagine being part of the outside world. His son would not need the outside world, either. He would teach his son to live simply, to love nature, to be independent. He'd make sure his son knew what was good and true...not money, not accolades, praise, success. But this island, this sky, this sea.

But perhaps the years of living so isolated had made him rough and impatient. He felt so very impatient now, waiting for her. She wasn't rushing her shower. She wasn't hurrying up to meet him. She was taking her time. Making him wait.

Finally the sound of the wooden door scraping the tumbled marble floor made him turn.

Georgia stepped outside, onto the terrace, her expression wary. She was dressed in black tights, a long black-and-white knit jumper, high-heeled ankle boots, and her shimmering blond hair was drawn back in a high ponytail. Even though she was wearing no makeup, she looked far more rested than she had earlier, but her guarded expression bothered him.

He didn't want to be a monster. He didn't enjoy scaring women. "You found it," he said gruffly.

"I did."

"Something to drink?" he asked, gesturing to the tray

with pitchers of water and juice that had been brought up earlier.

"Just water. Please."

He filled a tall glass and brought it to her. She was standing now where he'd been just seconds ago, looking out over the Aegean Sea. He wasn't surprised. The view was spectacular from the terrace, and the setting sun had gilded the horizon, turning everything purple and bronze.

"How are you feeling?" he asked.

"Fine," she said crisply, keeping her distance.

He should apologize. He wasn't sure where to begin, though. The words stuck in his throat. He wasn't very good at this sort of thing, and he was certain that the apology would be rebuffed.

"Do you get carsick easily?" he asked, trying to find a topic that would help them move forward.

"Not usually. Everything is different when you're pregnant, though."

"My pilots did say it was a turbulent landing. We get very strong winds this time of year." He hesitated. "I apologize."

She arched an elegant eyebrow, her expression cool. "You can't control the wind," she said, taking a sip of the water before adding, "But you can control yourself. Don't break down my door again. Please."

Nikos wasn't used to apologies, but he also wasn't accustomed to criticism. His temper flared. He battled it back down. "I've assured you that the door will be fixed."

"That's not the point. Your use of force was excessive. I'm sure there must be an intercom or house phone you could use next time you wish to check on me."

"Maybe you don't lock the door next time."

Her brows pulled. "I always lock my bedroom door."

"Even in your own home?"

"I live alone. I lock doors."

"Is Atlanta so very dangerous?"

"The world is dangerous." Her voice was cool, almost clinical. "If I don't lock my door, I can't sleep."

"You're safe here."

Her chin lifted, her smooth jaw firming as her gaze met his. "I'm not sure what that means."

He was baffled by her response. "You can relax here. Nothing will hurt you here."

"Does that include you?"

Nikos stiffened. He took a step away, glancing past her to the water, and yet all he could see was Elsa. Elsa, who had been afraid of everything he was.

"I wouldn't hurt you," he ground out, forcing his gaze back to Georgia. "The reason you are here now is that I want to ensure your safety. Your well-being is imperative to my son's well-being. You will have only the best of care on Kamari."

She stared back at him, blue eyes bright and clear, as well as thoughtful. She was weighing his words, assessing them for herself. "I don't need *care*. I need space and respect."

"Which you will have, along with proper *care*."

She continued to hold his gaze. "I am not sure your idea of proper care and mine are the same thing. In fact, I'm sure it's not. For me, proper care would have been remaining at home, close to my sister and obstetrician. I would have felt healthier and safer with my doctor and family nearby."

"I have hired the best obstetrician and pediatrician in Greece. Both will attend the delivery, and the obstetrician will see you once a month until you are close to delivery."

"I would have been happier at home, though."

"Once the newness wears off, I think you will find it quite restful here."

A spark flickered in her eyes. Her lips compressed. "I

don't think you're understanding what I'm saying. When I agreed to the surrogacy I never expected spending time here, with you. That wasn't part of the initial agreement. Indeed, I wouldn't have agreed to the surrogacy if I'd known that I had to spend the final trimester here. I'm not happy being here. This isn't good for me."

"You've been compensated for coming to Kamari, generously compensated."

"But money isn't everything." Her chin notched up. "And I am not going to have you throwing money in my face. It's rude and demeaning."

"But you chose to be a donor and surrogate for the money."

"I needed to pay for medical school for my sister and me, but I also wanted to do something good. And I have. I've created life. You can't put a price on that." Her voice suddenly cracked, and she looked away, her lower lip caught between her teeth.

He studied her beautiful profile, saw a hint of moisture in her eyes and wondered if they were real tears or if this was perhaps part of a game. He didn't trust tears, and it crossed his mind that she could be trying to manipulate him. It was possible. Elsa had taught him that.

"And you have no qualms about giving this precious life up?" he asked, unable to mask the ruthless edge in his voice. He was not the same man he'd been before Elsa. He doubted he'd ever be that man again.

Georgia made a soft, rough sound, and when she spoke again, her voice was husky. "It's your son, not mine."

"Your egg. Your womb."

Her lips curved faintly, but the smile didn't reach her eyes. "I am little more than a fertile garden. The soil doesn't weep when you sow or reap."

An interesting answer, he thought. She was an interesting woman. "The soil isn't a young female, either. Nurturing...maternal—"

"I'm not maternal," she said, cutting him off, her tone almost icy.

"And yet you're doing this to help provide for your sister."

"That's different. She is my family. She is already my responsibility. But I have no desire to ever have children of my own. No desire to add to that family, or assume more responsibilities."

"You may feel differently later."

She leaned forward, her expression intent. "Do you want me to feel differently later?"

He was shocked, not just by her words but by the way she moved in toward him. No one invaded his space. No one wanted to be near him. He intimidated women. He made people uncomfortable. And yet she leaned in, she challenged him, and after the shock faded, he understood why.

She wasn't timid. She wasn't weak. She was strong, and she was going to give him as good as he gave her.

He admired her boldness and her confidence. He admired strength and courage, but what she didn't realize was that her challenge just whetted his appetite.

He wasn't about to move back and give her distance and breathing room. He was going to move in. Get closer. Crowd her.

Not because he wanted to scare her, but her energy and resistance were waking him up, making him feel things he hadn't felt in forever. And yet what was good for him wouldn't necessarily be good for her.

He was troubled by his response to her. She fascinated him. And, yes, she looked like Elsa, but her personality was nothing like Elsa's. While Elsa had needed to be shielded, protected, Georgia charged at him, refusing to shy away from conflict.

He found her stimulating.

Refreshing.

But he should warn her. He ought to tell her that she was stirring the beast, rattling his cage. He should let her know that she wouldn't like it when he woke...that it was better, safer, smarter to keep him leashed, caged, dormant.

"Of course I don't want you to feel differently later," Nikos said now. "He is my son."

"Good. I am glad we are in complete agreement on that." She walked away from him then, heading to the sitting area under the thatched roof and taking a seat on the white slipcovered bench against the house.

He watched her cross her legs and sit back, the picture of calm and cool, but her air of calm, that cloak of control, jolted him. A shot of adrenaline. Another shot of hunger. But he needed to smash the desire, not encourage the response. Hungry wasn't good. Hungry would hurt her.

He walked slowly toward her, studying her expression. From across the terrace she exuded serenity, and yet as he neared he saw a flicker in her eyes. She wasn't sleepy or lazy. She was alert and very much on guard.

He dropped into a chair across from her, his long legs extending, taking some of her space. "In the car you asked me where I was going to raise my son." Nikos paused a moment, his gaze skimming her stunning features, dropping from her full pink lips down the elegant throat to the pulse he could see beating at the base of her neck. She was not as calm as she pretended to be. Not by a long shot. "Why did you ask?" he added.

Her shoulders twisted. "Curious."

"Curious about the life he'll live, or curious about me?"

She shrugged again, even more carelessly than before. "I was just making conversation. I'm sorry if I made you uncomfortable."

"I wasn't at all uncomfortable. I love Kamari, so it was

easy to answer. I will raise my son here. We will live here, and I will teach him about his family, his lineage, and make sure he is prepared to inherit the Panos business and fortune. He is my legacy. He is the future."

For a moment after he'd finished speaking there was just silence. It wasn't an easy silence. She was very much processing every word he was saying. Georgia Nielsen was no intellectual lightweight.

He gestured to her already nearly empty glass. "More water, Georgia?"

"I'm fine."

Yes, she was. She was actually more than fine, and it would be a problem if he didn't check his interest immediately. What they needed were boring topics. Safe subjects. And distance. "We Greeks like our water. We serve water with coffee, water with dessert. It's often the beverage of choice—" His voice was drowned out by the roar of an engine.

He fell silent as the white Falcon that had brought Georgia to the island flew directly overhead. Georgia's head tipped, and she watched the plane take off, soaring up into the sky.

"Your plane doesn't stay here?"

"No. The hangar's in Athens."

She was still watching the jet. He watched her, appreciating the elegant lines and delicate angles of her face. The gold of her hair. The cool blue-gray of her eyes. Her complexion wasn't pink but palest cream with just a hint of gold.

Elsa's complexion hadn't been honey, but pink and cream. Roses and porcelain. The blue of her eyes had been more violet. Her lips were smaller, her eyes set a little wider. Doll-like.

Georgia was nothing like a doll.

She turned her attention from the sky back to him. "Why Athens?"

"It's where I keep all of my planes."

"You have more?"

"Yes. Helicopters, too."

"Any boats?"

"Of course. I live on a remote island."

She pushed a blond tendril back from her brow. "Is it too late to tour the island now?"

"The sun will be setting in the next hour. It's better to wait for the morning. I'll show you the gardens, the walking paths and the pool. I imagine you'll want to get your exercise in." He rose and went to get the water pitcher and refill her glass. "Mr. Laurent said you exercise regularly. Is that still the case?"

"I walk, swim and cycle and lift weights—"

"No more weights."

She laughed, amused, the sound soft and husky. "We're not talking Olympic moves here."

"No weights," he repeated. "I don't think it's necessary to stress you, or the baby, that much."

She opened her mouth to protest but closed it, shrugged.

"The pool is heated," he added. "I think you'll find it quite pleasant."

She leaned all the way back against the cushion and extended her long legs. "Will it be this way for the next three and a half months?"

"What does that mean?"

"Will you be supervising my nutrition along with my exercise?"

He heard the mockery in her voice, and it didn't anger him as much as stir his senses. She had no idea how appealing he found her. He should warn her. If not for her sake then his. "Yes," he answered smoothly. "It will be this way." There was no point denying it. She was here so he could monitor the pregnancy and make sure the third trimester went well.

Her lips curved faintly. Amusement lurked in her eyes. "Then we have a problem."

"Not if you're compliant."

She gave him another long look, one perfect brow lifting. "And is that how Mr. Laurent described me? Docile... sweet...compliant?"

The air was suddenly charged, crackling with tension and resistance.

No, he couldn't imagine her ever being described as any of those, and he hadn't been throwing down a challenge, either, just setting forth his expectations. But she was turning his expectations into something more.

Heat rushed through him, hot and heavy in his veins. His body ached. His blood hummed. He was waking up. It felt far too good.

"I don't believe that was ever Mr. Laurent's description," Nikos replied gently, aware of the dance they were being drawn into. "I think my attorney used words like *intelligent, gifted, successful, ambitious.*"

Her blue gaze held his. She was looking so deeply, so directly, that he wondered what she was thinking...seeing. She didn't appear threatened. Didn't seem the least bit uneasy. If anything she radiated confidence. Control.

For being just twenty-four, Georgia Nielsen struck him as a powerful woman in her element.

Not the surrogate he'd expected. Not the surrogate he wanted.

But just possibly a woman he wanted.

Careful, he told himself. *Do not be stupid...do not complicate things...*

"I'm not accustomed to being told what to do," she said, her voice pitched low and firm. "And I might be your guest here for the next few months, but I am my own person."

And he wasn't accustomed to negotiating with anyone,

certainly not a woman. But he found it exciting. She was exciting. "Can you not think of it as care and concern for the well-being of my son?"

A light flickered in her eyes. "I have taken excellent care of him so far."

"I appreciate that. But as his father, I expect you to respect my wishes."

She stared back at him, unrepentant.

There was definitely a power struggle taking place. He hadn't anticipated that, either. She was carrying his son. She was hired to carry his son. All she had to do was heed his wishes. But it appeared that Georgia either couldn't, or wouldn't, and her resistance was like gasoline to a flame.

He wasn't angry. Not in the least. But his heart was thudding, and blood was drumming in his veins.

Nikos placed her glass on the corner table and sat back down across from her. "I think we have a misunderstanding." His tone was pleasant. There was no need to snarl. He knew just how dangerous he was…just how dangerous he could be. "Maybe it's a language barrier. Maybe it's cultural—you are American, I am Greek—but business is business. You entered into an arrangement with me, and I have met my end of the agreement. I have paid you, handsomely, for your service—"

"We are discussing my body. I am not a shipping container or a maritime vessel. I am not your employee, either. I am a woman who is giving you a gift—"

"Providing a service," he interrupted. "We have to call it what it is."

"Yes, the *gift* of life," she shot back, tone defiant, blue eyes blazing. "But I'm not just any woman. I'm the one you wanted to be both egg donor and surrogate. There was a reason you picked me. You could have picked any woman, but you selected me, which means you have me, and I am not going to be pushed around. I don't respect men who throw their weight around, either. You can have a conversation with me, but don't dictate to me."

For a long moment there was just silence.

Georgia felt the weight of Nikos's inspection. He wasn't happy. At all. She wasn't afraid, just alert. Aware. Aware of his intensity, and how energy seemed to crackle around him. He wasn't moving, and yet she could feel the air hum.

She'd never met anyone like him before. And if she weren't here, trapped on an isolated island with him, she'd be intrigued. She'd be tempted to test the fire and energy, but she was trapped here, and the survivalist in her told her she needed to be careful, and she needed to get off the island. Soon.

"Does no one else live on Kamari?" she asked, filling the taut silence.

"Just my staff."

"Are there many?"

"A half dozen or so, depending on the day and occasion."

"And do you ever leave here? Will we ever go anywhere?"

His mouth quirked, his dark eyes narrowing. "You've only been here a few hours. Are you already so anxious to leave?"

"I've never been to Greece."

"And here you are."

She smiled and glanced past him, her attention drawn to the blue horizon. "But I see other islands. They cannot be that far."

"The closest is Amorgós. It is twenty-six kilometers away."

"How do you get there?"

"I don't."

She allowed her smile to grow, stretch. "What if I wanted to visit?" she asked lightly.

"And why would you want to do that?"

"I might want to shop—"

"You want to buy olives…bread…soap? Because that is all the shops have there this time of year. It's not high season. In winter, Amorgós is not for tourists. It has a few small shops with meat and produce, but that is all."

"Surely there is more to the island than that."

His broad shoulders shifted. "There is a ferry, a hospital and a monastery—plus churches. Many churches. But no museums, no café culture, nothing that would appeal to you."

"You don't know me. How do you know what would appeal to me?"

"You are young and beautiful. Young, beautiful women like to have a good time."

She laughed, entertained. Or at least, it was what she'd have him think. The quickest way to lose control was to get emotional. "That is so incredibly sexist."

"Not sexist. I'm just honest. And before you think I am being unfair to the female gender, let me add that young, beautiful men like to have a good time, too."

"But not you."

"I am neither young nor beautiful."

"Are you fishing for compliments?"

He leaned forward so that they were just inches apart and stared deeply into her eyes. "Look at me."

Oh, she was, and this close his eyes weren't just dark brown, but rich chocolate ringed with a line of espresso. His lashes were black, thick, long, perfectly framing the rich brown irises. His black brows were strong slashes. "I'm looking," she said calmly, her cool voice belying the change in her pulse, her heart beginning to race. She didn't know what was happening, but it was hard to breathe. She was growing warm, too warm. It was no longer easy to concentrate. "And you are still young, and despite the scars, you are still beautiful."

The space between them, those precious inches, shimmered with heat and tension. Even the air felt charged. Georgia dragged in a breath, feeling feverish.

"Is this a game to you?" he growled.

"No."

"Then look again."

"I am. So tell me, what am I supposed to be seeing?"

He reached up, and shoved his dark hair back from his temple, revealing the swath of mottled skin. "*Now* look at them."

"I am. They are burns," she said, struggling to sound clinical and detached as she reached out and lightly traced the thickened scar tissue. "They extend three inches above your brow, into your hairline, and then follow your temple down to your ear and out to the top of your cheekbone." Her fingers shook as she drew her hand back. She curled her hand in her lap. "How long ago did it happen?"

"Five years."

"They've healed well."

"There were a number of reconstructive surgeries."

His words told her one thing, but his espresso eyes said something else. She was far too warm and unsettled to want to analyze what was happening.

Too much was happening, and much too fast.

She hadn't come to Kamari prepared for any of this... For him.

He was so overwhelming in every way. The sheer physicality of him—his height, his size, the width of his shoulders, the thick angle of his jaw—coupled with his electric energy was knocking her sideways, making it difficult to think.

The next three and a half months would be impossible if she didn't throw up some boundaries, get some control. Normally she wasn't easily intimidated, but Nikos Panos was getting under her skin. She needed space and distance, fast.

"I'm exhausted," she said, rising. "I think I should return to my room."

"You need to eat."

"Then perhaps you'd be so kind as to send something to my room for me? I'm dying to eat and crawl back into bed." She managed a small, tight smile. Seeing that he was about to protest, she added quickly, "I might as well sleep now, while I can. I understand it won't be easy towards the end of this next trimester."

His brow furrowed. He didn't seem happy with her decision, but after a moment he rose. "I'll walk you back."

"No need."

"You are a guest here, and you've only just arrived. I'll see you to your room. It'll give me a chance to check your door, make sure it has been repaired."

She couldn't argue with his logic, and if she was going to survive here, she'd need to acquiesce now and then. She might as well allow him to win small victories.

They went down a flight of stairs, passing through the gleaming white living room and then out into a whitewashed hall that reflected gold-and-red light from the row of windows overlooking the sea.

Rays of burnished gold fell on Nikos, highlighting the width of his shoulders and haloing his dark head with light. With the sunset illuminating his strong profile he looked like an oil painting come to life, or perhaps a page lifted from a book on the Greek gods. One of Zeus's immortal sons here on earth…

"My room is just down there," he said, nodding to a corridor. "Should you need anything later."

"I won't need anything," she said.

"But if there's an emergency."

"There won't be."

He stopped outside her room. Her door was closed. He gave a twist to the door handle. It opened soundlessly. He closed it again. It closed smoothly. "It seems to be working properly."

She stepped past him and checked the door herself. It opened and shut, but the paint was scraped clean in a spot. A bit of hardware was missing.

The lock had been removed.

Georgia turned to face him. "This is not all right."

"The door shuts."

"You had the lock taken off. I told you—"

"And I told you that I need to be able to reach you should there be an emergency," he ground out, silencing her. "If you cannot sleep without a locked door due to anxiety or fear of being attacked, then I will sleep in your room with you—"

"No. That will not happen."

"Then deal with an unlocked door, because those are your options." He towered over her, features hard. "I will have a tray sent to you now, and I will see you in the morning for the tour of the house and gardens."

CHAPTER FOUR

IT TOOK FOREVER for Georgia to fall asleep.

She'd only been in Greece a few hours and yet she was already wishing she'd never agreed to travel to Kamari. The money wasn't worth it—

She stopped herself there.

The money would be worth it, if she calmed down and focused. Getting upset wasn't going to help. She'd been through many difficult experiences in her life and she could handle this one.

With that said, it would have been better to have known more about Nikos Panos than she did. Mr. Laurent had told her a little bit about the Panos family when she'd been selected for the surrogacy. He'd explained that the Panos family's fortune was fairly recent, only since the end of World War II, and that they'd made their money rebuilding war-torn Europe, then branched from construction into shipping and from shipping into retail.

She did a little more research on her own at that point. The Panos story wasn't all sunshine and roses. The company had floundered during the past decade, poor investments and too much expansion in the wrong direction. Teetering on the brink of bankruptcy, son and heir Nikos Panos took the helm and turned the floundering company around.

Nikos's success had reassured her. She'd assumed he was successful and stable. She needed to learn not to make assumptions.

Or perhaps she needed to stop thinking about Nikos. Maybe she needed to practice detachment. And not just about Nikos, but the pregnancy, too.

She'd lost so much when her parents and sister and grandparents died. And now she had to be careful she didn't get her heart broken again. He wasn't her baby. He wasn't her son. Nor would he ever be.

Georgia finally fell asleep, but the morning came far too quickly. Waking, she frowned at the bright sunshine. She was not ready for the tour or more time with him.

Boundaries and distance, she told herself, showering and then dressing, choosing skinny jeans and an oversize gray cashmere sweater and gray ankle boots. The sky was clear, but her room was cold and outside the wind howled, buffeting the stone villa.

Boundaries and distance, she repeated when Nikos knocked at her bedroom door a few minutes later, coming to collect her personally for the morning tour.

It was a shock seeing him in the windowless hall, cloaked in shadows. He was wearing black trousers and a black shirt, and although she was tall, he towered over her, his broad shoulders filling the doorway, consuming space.

His dark gaze swept over her before focusing on her feet. "Please change the boots to something more practical."

She choked on an uncomfortable laugh, thinking he was joking, but he didn't laugh or smile. Her brows lifted, unable to believe they were starting a new day this way. "You're serious?"

"That's the third pair of boots. Heeled boots—"

"These are practically flats. The heel is maybe an inch tall."

"They are two inches or more, and you're not going to wear them and risk twisting an ankle or breaking your neck."

"I don't know what clumsy women you dated in the past—"

"We are not on a date. You are a surrogate. Change your shoes."

She laughed. She couldn't help it.

From the darkening of his expression, he hadn't expected that response, which made another bubble of laughter rise. She struggled to smash this one, too, but the sound escaped, and she bit the inside of her lip, trying to muffle her amusement and failing miserably.

Did he really expect her to jump to his bidding? Was he accustomed to women bowing and scraping?

Clearly he had no idea who *he* was dealing with. The Nielsen sisters were not pushovers. Neither Savannah nor Georgia were known to be quiet, timid, pliable women. The daughters of Norwegian American missionaries, they'd grown up overseas, moving with their parents from mission to mission, before losing their family in a horrific assault four years ago. Georgia and her sister had battled through the grief together and had emerged stronger than ever.

And Nikos should know that.

He'd selected *her* from thousands of egg donors and potential surrogates. Mr. Laurent told her that Nikos had examined her profile in great depth as he was very specific about what he wanted—age, birth date, height, weight, blood type, eye color, natural hair color, education, IQ.

"You laugh," Nikos said grimly.

"Yes, I did, and I will again if you continue to act as if you're a barbarian. I might be your *paid* surrogate, but I've a good brain, and I don't need you telling me what to do every time I turn around."

"Then your *good* brain and your *common* sense should tell you that wearing impractical shoes is asking for trouble."

"They are ankle boots, with a tiny stacked heel." She held up her fingers, showing him a sliver of space between her thumb and pointer finger. *"Tiny."*

His sigh was heavy and loud. "You are as exasperating as a child."

"I don't know how much experience you've had with children, but you do seem to be an expert in belittling women—"

"I'm not belittling women in general. We're discussing you."

"You might be surprised to discover that I don't want your attention. I don't want your company, either. You are insufferably arrogant. I completely understand why you live on a rock in the middle of the sea. Nobody wants to be your neighbor!"

"And I think you enjoy fighting."

"I don't enjoy fighting, but I'm not about to bow and scrape. I don't like conflict, but I won't let you, or anyone, bulldoze over me." She was breathing fast, and her hands knotted at her sides. "You started this, you know. You talk to me as if I'm feebleminded—"

"I'm helping you."

"You'd help me more by staying out of my business. I don't tell you how to eat or exercise. I don't tell you how to dress or what shoes to wear—"

"I'm not pregnant."

"No, I am—that's correct. And when I'm upset my blood pressure goes up and my hormones change and the baby feels all of it. Do you think it's good for your child when you get me all worked up? Or maybe since he is your son he enjoys a good fight."

Nikos scowled at her. "I don't enjoy a fight, and nor does he."

"Then if you don't enjoy a fight, don't provoke one."

"Maybe you are the one that needs to compromise."

"I am. I have. I'm here!" Georgia gestured to the room, the window, the view beyond. "I left my home to be your guest for three and a half months, and I've given up everything to make you happy. You can try to make me happy, Nikos."

He stretched out his arms, putting an elbow on either side of the plastered doorway, his shoulders forming a thick, muscular wall. He drew a slow, deep breath, his dark eyes burning, revealing his chaotic emotions. "We are not going to do this for the next three-plus months," he growled as a lock of his thick black hair fell forward, half hiding one dark eye, concealing the scars at his temple. "This is my home, my sanctuary. It's where I live to be calm and in control—"

"And would it hurt you so much to give up a little control?" she interrupted furiously. "Is it impossible for you to back off and just give me breathing room?"

"You only just arrived."

"Exactly. And yet you've already broken down my door—"

"Which I apologized for."

She snorted. "You didn't apologize. You just fixed it. But that's not an apology. And now you're hanging from my door, your giant body blocking my room, as you lecture me about calm and control while you act like a crazed werewolf—" She broke off, gulped air. "Mr. Laurent should have told me the whole story. He shouldn't have sold me on how smart and successful you were. He shouldn't have portrayed you to be this brilliant Greek tycoon. He should have told me the truth. You're a *nightmare*!"

Georgia knew immediately by the flare of hot white light in his eyes that she'd gone too far, said too much. But she was also in too deep, her emotions too stirred up to do anything but end the conversation as fast as she could.

"You're right," she added breathlessly. "This isn't working. Let's forget the tour. I'll find my way around. I think it's best if you just do your thing and let me do mine." And then she slammed the door shut, praying that as the door scraped shut, it didn't take off his face.

For a split second after Georgia closed the door, she felt wildly victorious. The rush of adrenaline was pure and strong, and she praised herself for handling the situation—and him—without revealing cowardice or weakness.

Perhaps he'd learn from this, she mentally added, heading toward the sitting area, where she'd piled her books. Perhaps he'd realize that his controlling boorish behavior was detrimental to the well-being of them all—

And then her door flew open, and he stormed across the threshold. Georgia's heart tumbled to her feet. All self-congratulating ended when she saw his livid expression.

She backed up a step, and then another as he continued to charge across the room. "What are you doing?" she cried, praying he didn't hear the wobble in her voice. "Get out! This is my room—"

"No, *gynaika mou*, it seems you are in need of a little lesson. This isn't your room. It's a room in my house that I am allowing you to use," he gritted out, marching toward her. "So to repeat, so we can be absolutely clear, this is my house. My room. You are *my* surrogate carrying *my* son."

Her heart drummed double time as he bore down on her but she wasn't about to retreat. "It might be your house, and the baby might be your son, but I am not *your* surrogate. I do not belong to you, and I will never be any man's possession."

"You took my money—"

"Not that again!"

"So until you give birth, you are mine."

"Wrong." She threw her shoulders back. "Not yours. I will never be yours. In fact, I'd like to call Mr. Laurent right now. I think it's time he and I had a little conversation and sorted things out."

"You don't need to call anyone."

"Oh, but I do. I've had enough of your hospitality and think I'd be more comfortable in a hotel somewhere in Athens—"

"That's not going to happen."

"You can't keep me here."

"But I can. You're my responsibility. You're in my care."

"Are you telling me that I can't leave?"

For a moment there was just silence. His jaw tightened. His dark eyes glowed, and then his lashes dropped, concealing his expression. "You are safe here," he said quietly. "Safer here than anywhere else in Greece."

"But I don't feel safe. You don't respect me, nor do you respect my need for distance and boundaries."

He frowned. "How am I not respecting your boundaries? I haven't touched you, haven't threatened you in any way."

"If you don't know what respect is, I am certainly not going to try to explain it to you. But it does renew my concern about staying here, living in such close proximity to you. Safety isn't just physical. It's psychological—"

"Renew your concern? What does that mean? You were not comfortable coming here?"

"Of course I wasn't comfortable. I didn't know you. I still don't. But what I've learned since arriving isn't flattering." She held his gaze. "I feel as if you and Mr. Laurent deliberately deceived me—"

"Deceived you how? Were you not paid? Were you not given an incredibly generous bonus for traveling here?"

"Now that I know you, it wasn't enough. In fact, I don't think you could have ever paid me enough to put up with your nonsense."

He threw his head back. "Nonsense?"

"Yes. You're behaving like a thug, a bully—"

"That's enough, *gynaika*."

She had no idea what he'd called her in Greek, but she

didn't particularly care, not when his tone and words were so insufferably patronizing. "I'd like to use your phone. I want to call Mr. Laurent."

"And what do you think Mr. Laurent is going to do?"

"Get me a plane ticket out of here."

"Mr. Laurent works for me. He is *my* attorney."

"He promised me…" Her voice faded, and she swallowed hard as she struggled to remember just what Mr. Laurent had promised. She drew a blank. Surely Mr. Laurent had promised her something…?

"And what did my attorney promise you, Georgia?" Nikos drawled, seeing her uncertainty.

She held her breath, fighting her nerves. Her heart hammered hard. "He said you were a good person. He said you could be trusted." She stared him in the eye. "And I believed him. And I believed in you. So, either you respect my wishes, and leave my room now, or I will know everything he said, and everything you are, is a lie."

Thank God her voice was clear, strong, authoritative. It was the right voice for emergencies.

And Nikos Panos was most definitely an emergency, especially when he stood toe to toe with her, hands clenched, jaw tight. His dark eyes continued to bore into her, scorching her, demanding her to back down. Acquiesce.

Georgia didn't acquiesce. *Ever.*

"No one speaks to me with such impertinence," he ground out.

"Perhaps if they did, you'd have better manners."

"Enough," he snapped, silencing her. "Enough with your words. The sound of your voice exhausts me. I am quite certain my son is fed up, as well." And then he walked out.

Georgia dropped onto the couch in the living room and curled her legs up under her, stunned. She felt as if she'd been through a major battle and she was wiped out.

Nikos Panos was not like any man she'd ever met before, and she sincerely hoped she'd never meet anyone like him again.

Even after sitting for several minutes she continued to shake. She wasn't afraid, just shell-shocked.

She couldn't believe his behavior. She couldn't imagine anyone acting that way, much less to the woman hired to carry his child.

How did he think she'd react when he threw his weight around, told her how to dress, how to behave?

A rap sounded on her door. She knew from the firm knock who it was.

"Yes?" she called, too worn-out to get off the couch.

The door opened, and Nikos stood on the threshold, looking not much happier than he had ten minutes ago when he'd stormed out.

"May I come in?" he asked with terse civility.

"If we're done fighting," she answered.

He entered her suite of rooms, walking toward her. "I don't enjoy it, either."

She arched a brow but didn't contradict him.

He paced the living room floor, up and back, his jaw hard, his glossy black hair tousled but still framing his handsome features perfectly.

When he wasn't talking and enraging her, he was a beautiful man.

"I am not a barbarian," he said at length. "I'm not a caveman or a werewolf." He turned, faced her, arms folded over his powerful chest. "I am just a man. That is all."

There was something different in his voice and eyes. Something almost vulnerable. She felt a peculiar ache in her chest, and she swallowed around the lump forming in her throat.

When he wasn't growling at her and stalking her and making her heart beat too fast, he was quite handsome, and just possibly a tiny bit appealing. But he growled and muttered and intimidated far more than necessary.

"I am sorry if I hurt your feelings," she said carefully, "but your world here isn't my world. Your life here—it's what you know—but it's all new for me. And it's not normal for me."

"I have never intended to disrespect you. I have merely tried to help you."

She nearly smiled at his idea of being helpful, and then her smile faded as she remembered his last words before he marched out. "I can forgive nearly all of it, but you were deliberately cruel when you said that your son was fed up with the sound of my voice."

He said nothing. He just looked at her.

A lump filled her throat, making it hard to swallow. Her eyes burned, and her heart felt so sore. If she wasn't careful, she'd cry, and she never cried. At least, she rarely cried, and she never cried in front of strangers. Or Savannah. She never wanted to frighten Savannah. Georgia prided herself on her strength.

Now she knotted her hands in her lap and blinked hard to clear her eyes. "You do know that your son lives in my body." She was fighting the lump in her throat now. It had doubled in size and was making it difficult to speak. "Your son doesn't even know you yet, Nikos. The only thing he knows right now is *me*. My voice. My heartbeat. And for your information, he likes both, quite a bit."

Nikos's jaw flexed, a tiny muscle bunching in his jaw, near his ear. "I'm certain he does," he said quietly. "I'm sure he thinks you're his mother."

The words, gently spoken, cut her to the quick.

The tears she'd fought to hold back now flooded her eyes, and she looked away and bit down ruthlessly into her lower lip, forcing her teeth into the soft skin, drawing blood to distract her from the pain Nikos had just caused.

He was right, of course.

Absolutely right.

And yet she had never once let herself think those words, or feel the power of them.

The baby would lose his mother, just as she had lost her mother...

It wasn't fair, not for him. Maybe not for any of them. But it was the decision she had made to help provide for her sister. It was the only thing she could think to do given their circumstances.

She blinked hard, fiercely, trying to dry the tears, praying he didn't see them.

"Which is why you are here," he added flatly. "To allow my son to know me, to become familiar with my voice, to establish a bond so that when you leave the hospital after delivery, he won't be in distress as he will have me...his father."

Nikos wasn't making things better. He was making it worse. And his words felt like he'd poured salt all over an open wound.

So the baby won't be in distress...

So that when you leave, he won't suffer...

For a second she couldn't catch her breath. Pain splintered in her heart, radiating in every direction.

She'd never gone here...to this place...

She'd never really let herself think of him, though, cognizant of the fact that the child wasn't hers. It had been almost too easy these past six months to remind herself of that as she wasn't the maternal type, that she'd never played house or cuddled dolls as a little girl, not like Savannah or Charlie, her youngest sister, who wouldn't go anywhere without a doll in the crook of her arm.

She'd constantly reminded herself that she was the tomboy. That she didn't need touch, didn't need cuddles, didn't need tenderness. No, she was tough. A tomboy. She'd always preferred to run and jump and swim. Growing up, she'd been happiest challenging others to races. She loved competition. She was good at all subjects and brilliant at math. She loved doing complicated problems in her head, loved solving equations, and once she began studying chemistry, she found another favorite subject.

Life made sense in a lab. Math made sense.

Emotions and the heart…those didn't make sense. Those couldn't be managed and controlled.

So no, she'd told herself she didn't want children. She told herself throughout the hormone treatments and egg retrieval that she hadn't inherited a maternal gene. She'd repeated this during the IVF transfer, focusing on her lack of patience and her inability to compromise and yield as reasons why she shouldn't be a mother.

And then when she got the call that she was pregnant, that the embryo transfer had taken hold, her fierce, tough heart missed a beat.

She'd felt shock and joy, and then she'd suppressed the joy and focused on the future. Her future in medicine.

Conceiving the baby had been a scientific act, one with predictable steps and measurable progress. Of course there were uncertainties, just as there were with every pregnancy, but so far the pregnancy had been smooth.

At least, she'd been able to pretend it was smooth. But now Nikos had lifted the lid on Pandora's box. The baby had become real. And she could say she wasn't maternal, but she suddenly feared for the baby, feared for the life he might have to live…

Without her.

Georgia drew a panicked breath. Her fingers lightly grazed her bump, as if reassuring the baby that all would be well. But truthfully, now that she was here, now that she saw where the child would grow up, and how he'd grow up, and who would raise him, she wasn't at all sure he would be okay.

This wasn't the life she'd imagined for him...not that she'd spent that much time imagining a future she wouldn't be part of, but she'd smashed her worries with a blind confidence that the child was part of an immensely wealthy family and he'd lead a privileged life.

She'd told herself he'd have the best of everything: education, opportunity, protection.

Now she wondered if that would be enough.

Stop. Stop, Georgia, stop. She couldn't think like this, couldn't go there in her head, either. She'd known from the beginning she wouldn't keep the baby; she'd known she had no say in his future. She was a vessel. She was nothing more than a womb. She'd signed away every right to him.

Not her child.

His.

"Are you crying?" he asked, sitting next to her on the couch.

"No." She was not a crier. She couldn't remember when she'd last wept in public over anything.

"You are," he contradicted, taking her chin and lifting her face to his inspection, his dark gaze scrutinizing every inch of her face, making her cheeks flush and her eyes sting and burn. "What is happening? One moment you are laughing—the next you are crying. I don't understand."

That made two of them. She didn't understand, either. "Maybe it's the jet lag."

He gazed at her intently, staring into her eyes, as if able to see all the way through her. "Or pregnancy hormones?"

She could feel the heat of his fingers on her jaw, and a sensitive prickling in her skin. She couldn't remember the last time a man touched her. She'd dated plenty but medical school had been so consuming for the past few years that there was no time for serious relationships, and even if Georgia had time, she wasn't one to jump in and out of bed. It wasn't her upbringing—she wasn't pious in the least—but trust. Or lack of trust. She wasn't comfortable stripping bare, becoming vulnerable. She wasn't comfortable exposing her body or her heart.

"Emotions are definitely more volatile when pregnant," she conceded, trying to ignore the crazy pulse leaping in response, wondering if he could feel the rapid staccato in her jaw, hoping he couldn't, as the mad beating of her heart wasn't due to fear, but something else…something worse.

She was reacting to him. Responding to him.

"I am not usually emotional," she added.

"So you said on the application."

"I'm not," she insisted. "It's you. Your effect on me."

His brow furrowed. "Are you afraid of me?"

"No. Not afraid. But you are intense. I'm sure I'd be calm…or calmer…if you gave me a little bit more space." She'd tried to sound matter-of-fact, but the words came out breathless, her voice suddenly pitched low and husky.

He heard the husky note, and a light entered his dark eyes. His hand slipped from her jaw, sliding down over her neck, and her lips parted in a silent gasp.

She didn't like him, but clearly some part of her liked his touch. Pleasure rippled through her.

She didn't know if he'd heard her gasp, or felt her shiver, but his gaze focused on her mouth, and his fingertips lightly stroked her neck, as if intent on discovering just how she'd been wired.

The problem was, she'd been wired very well. She'd always been a little too physically sensitive. A little too aware of pleasure. And pleasure coursed through her. She gasped again, no longer connected by muscle and bone, but by nerves and sensation. Shocking to think that some twisted part of her enjoyed his touch.

"You are not the surrogate I believed I was getting,"

he said, drawing his hand back, but not before his finger-tips grazed her collarbone, sending another little flurry of sparks shooting through her.

She longed to fall back, needing air and space and oxygen, but her feet felt leaden and her brain was fuzzy. "I will change those shoes," she said faintly. "Shall I meet you outside?"

"I'll wait by the door."

"Nikos, I'm not going to fall as I change my shoes."

"And I'm not taking chances."

The villa was a large, broad three-story square building that appeared to be attached to the mountain, as if it had grown from the volcanic rock jutting from the sea. The foundation of the villa went all the way down into the water, and each of the three floors above the foundation had access to a different outdoor terrace.

Georgia could tell that someone, at some point, had attempted to turn the collection of rooms into habitable space with a slap of plaster and a wash of white paint. The worn plaster might have had more charm if so many of the rooms weren't cold. There were moments during the tour that Georgia was certain that it was warmer outside than inside. Clearly, this was not the Greece of travel brochures. Or at least, not modern Greece.

"Originally this was a fortress and then a medieval merchant's warehouse and then, during the Renaissance, a monastery. Now it is just my home," Nikos told her as they left the formal dining room and entered what had to have been a chapel and was now a room lined with bookshelves. The soaring vaulted ceiling gave the room a spaciousness that was lacking elsewhere. "My library," he said. Then adding, "You're welcome to study here."

She appreciated the offer, thinking she would enjoy studying here, and not just for the room's beauty but for its comfort. The large ceramic-glazed heater in the corner was making the library toasty warm.

After leaving the house, Nikos showed her the gardens. There weren't many shrubs and plants in the ground, as there was little rainfall in this part of the Cyclades, just a half-dozen potted bougainvillea close to the house and a scattering of gnarled cypress trees farther away, dotting the numerous walking paths.

Nikos escorted her on the various paths, wanting her to be comfortable with each. Some of the paths were laid with stones, others were packed with crushed gravel. Nearly all had a bench somewhere, providing a place to sit and enjoy the stunning views of the sea, dotted with distant islands.

Georgia would never tell Nikos, but she was glad he'd had her change into proper walking shoes, and it felt good to walk and stretch her muscles and breathe in the fresh, brisk air.

Twenty minutes after setting off, they returned to the villa, passing through a different walled garden on the third level to reach the house. She'd expected more benches, or perhaps a table and chairs, but instead there was an enormous outdoor pool, the water a sparkling aquamarine, glinting beneath the sun. The pool had lane lines for lap swimming as well as broad steps in a corner of the shallow end. Padded lounge chairs flanked both ends and pots of lemon trees dotted the courtyard, while a burst of red bougainvillea clung to one dazzling white wall.

It was lovely and so inviting. It was the kind of pool one would see at a very exclusive resort and yet Nikos had it all to himself. "You said last night that you keep it heated," she said.

He nodded. "I love the water and like to swim year-round." He walked her to the little whitewashed, tiled-roof pool house at the far end. "Towels, robes, shower and a sauna," he said. "Although the sauna is off-limits for you."

She shot him a reproving glance. "You don't need to do that. I am very much aware of what I should and shouldn't do during a pregnancy."

"Because you're a med student?"

"Because I've been reading all the books and researching what I don't know, and listening to what my doctor tells me. Most of it is common sense anyway." She dug her hands into the back pocket of her jeans. "But speaking of medical school, I do need to get some studying done. I tried during the flight but wasn't very successful."

"Mr. Laurent said your exam was scheduled for late June. But isn't that pushing it a bit, considering you'll be delivering late May, or possibly early June?"

"I should be fine. Provided I study."

He took her back then, past the pool, into the house and then down the stairs to the second floor, where their bedrooms were. They were silent as they walked, their footsteps ringing on the hard tumbled marble floor, passing through whitewashed halls with brief glimpses out the windows at the startlingly blue sky and sea. She felt Nikos's mood change as they walked, and she darted a glance at him, wondering what had happened to make the silence feel dark and brooding.

She needed to understand him, or the next three and a half months would be beyond miserable.

"Why are you doing this?" she asked as they reached her bedroom door. "Surely there are better, easier, as well as cheaper, ways to become a father."

"I want a child, not a wife."

"Are wives such awful things?" She was trying to be light and funny but he didn't smile.

"I was married. Marriage isn't for me."

"Maybe a different wife—"

"No." His expression hardened. "I'm not marriage material. I do not make a good husband."

"Your edges can be rough, but you're not all bad. You're quite protective, maybe overly protective—"

"You haven't seen the real me."

"No?"

"No."

She should have felt trepidation then, but she didn't. Instead he'd simply made her curious. He reminded her of a puzzle or equation that wanted solving. "What is the real you like?"

He hesitated a long moment. "Aggressive." His dark eyes found hers and held. "Carnal."

His answer, in that deep, rough voice, sent a rush of heat through her. *Carnal.*

She couldn't remember the last time she'd heard anyone use that word. It was such a biblical word…

Her mind scrambled to think of something to say even as her mouth went dry and her body grew hot, skin prickling, every inch of her suddenly painfully sensitive.

Before she could think of an appropriate response, he nodded and was gone, heading back down the hall.

CHAPTER FIVE

NIKOS WALKED SWIFTLY down the hall, his right hand squeezed into a fist. He couldn't get away from Georgia's rooms fast enough.

He knew why he'd told her those things about himself. It had meant to be a warning, to ensure she kept her distance, but his words hadn't scared her.

If anything, the warning had the opposite effect. She'd looked at him with her wide, thoughtful eyes, her expression intrigued.

But she shouldn't be intrigued. She needed to know who she was dealing with…what she was dealing with…

He'd scarred Elsa—broken her—and he didn't want to ever hurt another woman in the same way. He'd sworn off women. Sworn off love and passion. But he was determined to be a father, determined to break the curse, if there really was a curse…

Maybe then the wounds would heal.

Maybe there would be more. A future. New life.

Three and a half months until his son was here. Three and a half months until he could close the door on the past. And Elsa.

Once the baby was here, there would be no Elsa and no grief. There would be hope. And yet it hadn't been easy getting to this point. There had been so many dark moments and endless nights.

He might be the devil incarnate, but apparently even the devil could be a father. And he'd wanted to be a father since he was a boy. He'd wanted a family, maybe because he'd been so lonely as a boy. He'd married Elsa certain there would be children, but it hadn't worked out that way.

* * *

Nikos kept his distance the next day, aware that she had her studies to occupy her attention and he had his business.

But late in the afternoon he sent word to her room that he'd see her at five on the terrace for drinks and a lite bite, and then dinner would be at ten.

She was already on the terrace when he arrived, dressed in peach-and-gray cashmere. Her long hair had been braided into a simple side plait, with a couple of long golden strands loose to frame her face. He glanced down at her feet. Gray ankle boots. Small one-inch heel.

If he'd told Elsa no heels, she would have never worn anything but flats for the rest of their marriage. Clearly Georgia was no Elsa.

He nearly smiled, not sure why he was amused. Maybe it was just the relief that Georgia wasn't Elsa.

But before he could greet Georgia or offer her a drink, she lifted her laptop from the couch and approached him with it. "I haven't been able to figure out how to get on the internet," she said. "I am hoping you know the trick, or maybe it's password-protected."

"There isn't a trick," he said. "I don't really have reliable internet. It's satellite based, so imagine old-fashioned dial-up speeds and endless dropped file downloads, coupled with information darkness that lasts for hours, or worse, days."

He saw her jaw drop and eyes widen. "How do you go online?"

"I don't."

"At all?"

"Rarely."

"How can that be? I live on the internet. I use it for everything."

He shrugged. "When you don't have access to it, you learn to live without it."

"But in Athens you must have it."

"Yes."

"But why not here?"

"Greece has over six thousand islands and islets, and only two hundred and twenty-seven are populated. And where we are, in the Cyclades, there are very few people living. The Greek government can't afford to put in the cables and fiber optics needed for reliable and fast internet, and I'm certainly not going to pay for it, either."

"So how do you manage your business from Kamari without the internet?"

"I have a phone for meetings and emergencies, and once a week mail arrives—more frequently if something is urgent—and I'm quite happy with that."

Clearly she wasn't happy with the news. Her brows flattened, and she pursed her lips and studied him as if he were a dinosaur...or worse.

"I thought Mr. Laurent warned you," he said. "I asked him to prepare you. You were to have brought textbooks and whatever you could download onto your computer's hard drive—"

"I did do that."

"So you can study."

"Yes, but so many resources are online."

He shrugged again. "I guess you will have to do it the old-school way."

Her blue eyes blazed. "This isn't a game. This is serious."

"I'm not mocking you. I'm stating a reality. There is no internet. You need to rely on hard copies of everything."

She turned away from him, eyes closing for a moment, and then she drew a slow breath, as if trying to compose herself. "I also noticed you don't have TV or radio," she said quietly. "Is that true, or did I just miss seeing where you'd stashed them?"

"You are correct. I do not have TV or radio here."

Georgia walked to the white slipcovered couch and sat down, cradling her laptop against her. "You have nothing here for diversion."

She looked so stricken that he almost felt sorry for her. "I don't need it," he answered. "I like my thoughts. I read. I work."

"You're a hermit."

"I like the quiet, yes."

Georgia hugged the laptop closer to her. "It's rather frightening how isolated you are."

"It's not frightening, and you know I have a satellite phone when I need it."

He went to the tray with the pitchers of water and juice. "Want something?"

"Yes. A ticket to Athens, please."

His brow quirked. "Is that a name of an American cocktail?"

She gave him a long look. "You know it's not."

"What can I pour for you?"

"I'm not thirsty."

"You'll feel better if you stay hydrated, and this one is really good." He filled a tall glass and carried it to her. "Pomegranate juice and something else."

She took the glass from him and set it on the table next to her without drinking. "And you really never leave here?"

"Haven't in a year."

"What about when you…did your part…to make the baby?"

"The medical team came here."

"And what about when I need a checkup? In Atlanta, I saw the obstetrician once a month, just to make sure the baby was doing well. Will I really have that here, or are you just placating me?"

"Not placating you. The doctor will come here every four weeks to check on you, and the baby."

"You can afford to fly your doctor in, but you can't afford internet?"

"Laying fiber optics can cost millions to billions of dollars. Having a doctor make a house call is a lot less." He studied her a long minute. "Is it really so tragic not having access to the internet? Does it feel like a punishment to be so far removed from society?"

She was silent even longer, and then she reached for her juice glass and took a sip, and then another. "This is good," she said. "And unlike most American girls, I grew up without internet and TV and radio. We were lucky just to have electricity sometimes. There aren't many bells and whistles when you're the daughter of missionaries."

"So you can survive here without."

"Of course I can. The lack of internet will not break me. It's more of an issue of do I want to be without the internet? And the answer is no."

"You'll get used to it."

"Just like people get used to jail."

It was his turn to look at her hard. She blinked at him, wide-eyed innocence, and then smiled.

And her smile was not at all innocent.

It had been quite the day. Georgia practically drooped as she ate dinner. She wasn't hungry. She was too exhausted and numb to be hungry. But she couldn't call it a night until she'd exacted a promise from Nikos.

She wanted the lock put back on her door.

Was she afraid that Nikos would attack her in the night? No.

But she wasn't yet comfortable in the old villa and she would feel better with a door that locked. It'd give her a sense of security here, as well as a feeling of control.

She'd given up her world to come to Greece. How could he not make this concession for her? And Georgia didn't know if it was a birth-order thing, or just a survivor thing, but control was important to her. It was why she'd agreed to be a donor... She felt as if she was the one with control.

The surrogacy was another matter.

In hindsight it was a terrible mistake, but she was too tired tonight to go there and think about that. The only way she'd get through this last trimester was by just living one day at a time.

Nikos watched Georgia from across the dinner table, taking in the way the flickering candlelight illuminated her face, creating arcs of gold light as well as mysterious shadows and hollows.

It had been a tense cocktail hour, but dinner ended up being surprisingly relaxed. There wasn't a great deal of conversation during the meal, but Nikos didn't think Georgia minded the quiet. She didn't strike him as a woman who needed to constantly be chattering. He wasn't sure if that was because of the way she was raised or her own personality, but either way, he was grateful. He wasn't one who needed endless talk and conversation.

Early in his marriage, Elsa had somehow interpreted his silence to mean he was angry or upset. It created tremendous friction between them, and he'd tried to explain that he'd been a loner since he was a young boy, an only child in a small, strict family.

Unlike traditional Greek families, with lots of cousins and aunts and uncles, it was just his parents and him, and a grandfather even less inclined to talk than his father, forcing him to learn how to entertain himself, teaching him how to be his own friend. By the time he was a teenager, he was comfortable with his thoughts. The quiet gave him a chance to sort out problems—like how to help save the family business. His father wasn't a born leader, nor a savvy businessman, and when Nikos was still young, his father took bad advice from the wrong people and made a series of horrible decisions.

Those horrible decisions resulted in Nikos's father over-extending the company, investing in the wrong things and threatening to bankrupt them all when the entire country's economy crumbled.

If it hadn't been for Nikos's aggressive plan, Panos Enterprise would have been carved up and sold off to the highest bidder, leaving the family embarrassed and broke.

Nikos was twenty-four when he took over at Panos. Twenty-six when he married Elsa, and a widower at twenty-eight.

After Elsa's death he'd retreated here to Kamari, and he'd been living in virtual isolation for the past five years. He hadn't attended a wedding or a social occasion since Elsa's death.

He'd stopped traveling, too, as his burns drew attention and he didn't want to be stared at, didn't want to hear the whispers that would accompany his appearance somewhere. Once a year he forced himself to show up at the Panos headquarters in Athens, but the rest of the time, he flew his management in for meetings on Kamari.

There were no women in the upper management of his company, and that was deliberate, too, as he never wanted to be accused of forcing himself on women, nor did he want women whispering about his face.

He knew he was scarred.

He knew what people said about him.

Beast. Monster. Animal.

Werewolf. *Lykánthropos.*

Georgia's words came back to haunt him. He swallowed quickly and glanced past her, looking to the dining room window with the view of the moonlight reflecting off the sea.

Lykánthropos. That was a new one. He'd have to remember it and one day share a good laugh with his son.

"Nikos."

Hearing his name, he turned his attention back to Georgia. She was leaning toward him, her silken hair spilling over her shoulders, gleaming in the candlelight.

"Yes?" he said, sensing that all the calm was about to change.

"I want a lock for my door, Nikos." Her voice was quiet and steady but at the same time determined. She wasn't asking a question. She wasn't pleading. She was making a statement. A demand.

He tensed, his ease vanishing. So there was going to be drama after all.

He groaned inwardly, wishing Mr. Laurent had been more honest with him. The Atlanta attorney had made Georgia out to be a paragon of female intelligence and beauty, a combination of Athena and Aphrodite. Mr. Laurent had it wrong. Maybe he didn't know his goddesses, because Georgia was more like Artemis than Athena or Aphrodite. Artemis was the most independent spirit, and was known as the goddess of the hunt, nature and birth.

"We discussed this yesterday," he said, rolling the heavy silver napkin ring between his palm and the table. "You know why I don't want you to have a locked door."

"And I need you to understand why I want a lock on my door. I know it doesn't make sense to you—most men don't understand—but I won't sleep if I don't feel safe. And I don't feel safe—"

"Even though there is nothing here that can hurt you?"

"Surely you have irrational fears. Surely you understand that it's not about reality but about perception. Having a lock on my door gives me a sense of control, and that sense of control allows me to feel safer."

"I am not belittling your fears. You know why I removed the lock. I must be able to reach you if there's an emergency."

"You managed to kick the door down last time." Her lips curved, but the smile didn't reach her eyes. "And I'm sure if there was a real emergency, you could do it again."

"I was lucky that first day."

She reached across the table and touched his hand. *"Please."*

He flinched at the shock of her skin against his. Sparks shot through him, and his groin tightened. His gaze dropped to her hand resting on his. Her hand was pale against his skin, her fingers slender and narrow. He pictured stripping her tunic off, pictured the pale honey of her skin as she lay stretched naked in his bed.

He ground his teeth together, his molars clamped tight.

Georgia made him want things…made him want to do things…fierce, hard, hot. All the things that Elsa hadn't wanted. All the things sweet, gentle Elsa had been afraid of. Sex. Passion. Skin.

Carefully he disengaged, drawing his hand free of Georgia's. He struggled to organize his thoughts. She'd caught him completely off guard. And it wasn't just the touch, but her fearlessness.

Artemis.

He ached from head to foot, throbbing with sensation, his body hot with desire, the desire so new after so many years of feeling nothing, feeling dead.

Maybe a locked door would be a good thing.

"You could have a key," she added quietly. "In case of an emergency."

He looked up at her, and she was watching him intently,

her blue gaze unblinking. "But only you," she added. "No one else. I trust no one else."

He almost laughed. "You trust me?"

"You're the father of my b—" She broke off, swallowed. "This baby. I have to trust you. Don't I?"

The lock was installed that very night.

It was past midnight when Georgia finally went to bed, but she slept well. There were no bad dreams. There were no dreams at all, thank God.

But Nikos couldn't sleep.

He spent hours castigating himself. He shouldn't have brought her here. He should have waited until the very end of the pregnancy, and then arranged for Georgia to give birth in Athens. That would have been the way to go. That might still be the way to go. Have his plane come pick her up and send her to live at his house in Athens. His staff would care for her, and she'd be comfortable there—probably far more comfortable than here. She could shop and relax, attend the theater and eat good meals out.

But he wouldn't be there, and he wouldn't be able to keep an eye on her.

He wouldn't be able to protect her if things went wrong.

Which was why he'd brought her to Kamari.

What he needed to do was smash the desire. He had to control the attraction, and he could, if he just kept Elsa in his mind.

He'd crushed Elsa. He couldn't do that to Georgia.

The next morning when Georgia woke, she was grateful she'd slept well, but she couldn't quite smash the little anxious voice inside her, the one that kept reminding her of what she'd almost said last night at dinner.

My baby.

She'd caught herself in time, and didn't think Nikos had

noticed the slip, or her swift substitution, but she had, and it was eating at her.

This was a problem.

Why had she even thought the words? *My baby...?*

Where had that possessive pronoun come from? It had never been her baby... It wasn't ever going to be her baby. She didn't even like referring to the child as a he, preferring the impersonal "it" as a way of keeping distance... remaining detached.

Now she worried she wasn't quite as detached as she'd imagined.

Determined to silence the nagging voice, Georgia pushed the button that alerted the staff that she was awake. When one of the housemaids appeared at her door, Georgia asked for a light breakfast so she could start studying.

A tray arrived fifteen minutes later filled with bowls and dishes—thick, creamy yogurt, sliced fruit, warm pastries and an impressive silver pot of coffee.

Georgia ate at the little table in her living room, and then she set the tray aside and grabbed her books. She studied at the table all morning, and then at noon took a break to go to the pool to swim. She had swum yesterday and had managed thirty laps. Today she wanted to see if she could do forty, hoping the extra exercise would quiet her anxiety. She was right to have been worried about being here on Kamari for the third trimester. It wasn't going to be easy. She didn't feel calm or secure.

Hoping it was just hormones, she retrieved her goggles and kickboard from the pool house and began her swim.

She was halfway through her laps and paused at the wall to catch her breath. As she lifted her swim goggles, she spotted Nikos diving in the other end of the pool.

She caught only a glimpse of his body before he disappeared into the water, but he was in amazing shape—well built and tan, with hard, cut muscles everywhere.

He swam underwater halfway down the pool to finally surface on his back. Nikos did a couple of easy strokes, showing impressive form, before flipping over onto his stomach to continue down the pool, toward her.

Georgia felt a flutter of nerves and quickly pulled her goggles into place and set off down her lane. It was a big pool, and the white lane line divided the length into sides. He wasn't in her side, he'd taken the empty lane, but that didn't calm her down. Even though there was plenty of room for both of them, she felt increasingly self-conscious, especially when she could see him pass on the other side, his big bronze body slicing through the water.

He was a very good swimmer, a very strong swimmer. Gradually Georgia found herself watching him instead of continuing with her own laps.

He'd only just gotten in but he'd already swum six laps, making quick progress with his dark head down, his stroke smooth and steady. He had that kind of kick that was powerful without creating lots of splashing.

Each time he reached the wall, he did a neat flip turn, pushing off the tiles to glide beneath the water, before surfacing midway down the pool to continue swimming to the end.

She was impressed. He had to have once been a competitive swimmer.

Intrigued, Georgia grabbed her kickboard and began kicking her way down the pool, keeping her chin tucked in the water to try to hide the fact that she was watching Nikos.

She liked that he wasn't paying her any attention. She enjoyed just looking at him, studying his muscles and the way they bunched and tightened as he sliced through the water. From his tanned skin it was obvious he swam often, and he kept swimming for the next thirty minutes.

Georgia gave up, though. She found it too distracting to

have him there. She was heading for the steps when Nikos suddenly appeared at her side.

"All done?" he asked.

She sat down quickly on the middle step, the warm water lapping at her shoulders, hiding her figure. She wasn't usually prudish, but she felt almost naked in the suit, which was difficult when your body no longer felt like your body. Her breasts were so much fuller. Her belly was rounded. Every inch of her skin prickled, sensitive.

"Yes." She was nervous, and she didn't even know why. "Do you swim daily?" she added, trying to fill the silence.

"I try to. I like that it's something I can do year-round."

"You're good."

"I'm calmer after a swim. I find it's good to work off aggression and tension."

She studied his profile. She was beginning to realize that he was always careful to present her with the side of his face that wasn't scarred. That made her feel a pang of sorrow. He was so aware of how he looked to others, so aware that his scars must be unpleasant to others.

"Were you always…aggressive?" she asked, using his word, not sure if it was truly the right word for him. The more she got to know of him, the less aggressive she found him. He struck her as a man who was protective and prideful, but what man wasn't?

"No." He flashed white teeth. "I was quite shy as a boy. Painfully introverted."

"What changed you?"

He opened his mouth to answer and then changed his mind, giving her a shrug instead.

"Something must have happened," she persisted.

"I grew up. Became a man."

She wanted to reach out and turn his face. She wanted to see the pink scars, see where they disappeared into his hairline, and how they changed the hairline, and how they curved over his ear. She suspected he wore his hair loose and long to hide as much of the scars as he could.

"If your son inherits your good looks, he will be very lucky," she said with a smile.

Nikos frowned and looked at her quickly, his expression shuttered. "Is that a joke?"

She blinked in surprise. "No. You're very, very good-looking, Nikos—"

"You are pulling my leg."

"I'm not."

"I know what I am." His dark gaze met hers. "I know what you called me. *Lykánthropos.*" The edge of his mouth curled up. "That was a first, but it fits."

"I don't know what you just said."

"Werewolf." He was still smiling, but the smile hurt her. It was so hard and fierce and yet behind the smile she sensed a world of pain.

"I didn't mean it like that," she whispered, feeling a pang of guilt and shame. "It had nothing to do with your scars."

"It's okay. As I said, it fits."

"That's not why I said it."

"I've heard worse—"

"Nikos." She could barely say his name. Her heart hurt. "It wasn't your face. It's not the scars. It's the way you were hanging on my door, filling the space up. Your energy was just so big, so physical. You are so physical…" Her voice faded as she could see he wasn't even listening to her. "I'm sorry."

"Don't be. Now you know why I swim. I have a lot of energy. I've been told that I come across as very physical, and it's unpleasant for others. I don't want to be unpleasant for others. I wasn't raised to make women uncomfortable."

For a moment she couldn't speak or breathe. Her eyes stung, hot and gritty. Her heart felt impossibly tender.

Somehow everything had changed between them. Somehow she felt as though she were the aggressor and she was hunting him, chasing him with a pitchfork…

"I have a feeling you've been labeled unfairly," she said when she was sure she could speak. "I don't know that you are as aggressive as you think you are. In fact, I would say you are more protective than aggressive."

"That's because you don't know me well."

"What do you do that is so aggressive?"

"I have a forceful personality."

"This is true. But what specifically do you do that warrants the label? Do you yell…hit…punch…shake? Do you threaten women—"

"No! None of that. That is terrible."

"So what do you do? Are you hostile towards people? Antagonistic?"

"I try to avoid most people. That's why I live here. Works out better for everyone."

"And yet even here, you have to swim to manage your aggression and tension?"

"Maybe I should have said that swimming helps me burn off excess energy."

"That does sound better than aggressive." The wind blew across the pool and Georgia slid lower under the water to stay warm. "You and I have clashed, and I don't agree with some of your rules, including recommended footwear, but I wouldn't describe you as a hostile person. I'd say you're assertive."

"But in English, are they not the same things—aggressive and assertive?"

"For me, they are different. Assertive means being direct and strong, and, yes, forceful, but in a commanding sort of way, whereas I view aggressive to be far more negative. Aggressive can imply a lack of control, as well as unpleasantly hostile."

His mouth quirked. "Based on your definition, I would prefer to be assertive instead of aggressive."

She was thinking hard now on the word, and the various ways it could be used in the English language, and aggressive wasn't always negative. In fact, in medicine, an aggressive treatment was often the best treatment. "You know, aggressive can mean dynamic. In battle, you want to be aggressive. When dealing with cancer, you need an aggressive plan of attack."

"Sounds as if you are giving me permission to be aggressive."

She pushed at the water, creating small waves. "If it's for the right reason." She gave another push at the water, sending more ripples across the pool. "In business, I would think you'd have to be aggressive. Successful businesses are rarely complacent. I'm quite sure successful people are the same."

He ran a hand over his inky-black hair, muscles bunching and rippling in his bicep and shoulder. "You keep surprising me." His voice was rough, deep. "You're not what I expected. You are more." His head turned, and she glimpsed the scars he always tried so hard to hide. "My son is lucky to have had you as his...mother."

Georgia felt a lance of pain, her chest squeezing, air bottling. She struggled to smile, hiding the hurt as well as the wash of panic.

Mother...his mother...

Why did Nikos say that? Why would he say that? Something buried deep inside her wanted to scream, punch, lash out.

She wasn't this child's mother. She wasn't his mother. She wasn't. She'd signed those rights away forever, and it was the right thing to do. She wasn't prepared to be a mother, and certainly not a single mother who was only halfway through medical school.

Georgia rose and climbed from the pool. It was chilly out and shivering; she grabbed her towel and thick terry-cloth robe. The entire time she blotted herself dry she fought for calm and control.

She was someone who liked control, *needed* control, and yet she'd agreed to a contract that gave her no control…and was starting to turn her heart inside out.

Dropping the towel, Georgia quickly slid her arms into the robe, tying the sash around her waist, determined to get a grip. She couldn't panic. It wouldn't help to panic.

"I'll see you later tonight," she said to Nikos before rushing away. She dropped the damp towel in the laundry hamper at the pool house and then continued up to her room.

Her teeth chattered as she walked. She was scared. She didn't like this feeling. The pregnancy had changed everything, including her.

Her senses of taste and smell were different. Her emotions were more intense, and her moods were more volatile.

And now she was here, on a private island, in the middle of the Aegean Sea, with no phone and no internet and no way to distract herself from what was happening. And what was happening was beginning to rattle her.

She was having a baby, and then she was giving the baby away, before going away herself.

Good God. What had she done?

And why had she thought this was something she could actually do?

CHAPTER SIX

IT HAD BECOME custom to meet at sunset for drinks on the terrace. Quite often it was their first time seeing each other each day. Today had been different. They'd met at the pool during her swim and now they were together again, outside on the terrace on the third floor, taking in the sunset, making pleasant but inane conversation. She hoped the meaningless words would keep her from thinking, or feeling, because she was scared.

It was too late to have regrets. Too late to wish she'd never agreed to be a surrogate. An egg donor was one thing, but to carry the child, and then fly halfway across the world to deliver him in a foreign country?

And then leave him behind with a billionaire father who was both reclusive and eccentric?

It was a lot to digest, even for her.

Disruptive little thoughts had needled her all afternoon.

Her parents would be heartbroken if they knew what she was doing. And then there was Savannah, who'd been convinced from the outset that this would end badly. Savannah hadn't been as concerned about Georgia being an egg donor since a number of female medical students considered it an opportunity to do something good while improving their situation financially, but surrogacy was another matter.

And now Georgia was worried she'd completely lost sight of the big picture.

She'd agreed to this arrangement because it would provide a future for her and Savannah, but the future was becoming cloudy. Georgia felt emotional and confused. It wasn't a good combination. She had to get hold of her thoughts now. She needed to exert some control. It would be foolish, not to mention dangerous, to let the pregnancy hormones do her in. She had to remember her goals, focus on the objectives. There was a lot to come: the exam this summer, the rest of medical school, the right residency at the right hospital.

"More juice?" Nikos asked, interrupting her circular thoughts.

She lifted the special juice cocktail the cook had prepared for her—blood orange juice and sparkling water—and saw it was nearly gone. Beyond her glass, the sky burned, glowing with fiery orange and burnished gold.

"I'm fine, thank you," she said, gaze riveted now to the horizon, transfixed by the sun dropping into the sea. "What an incredible sunset. Every night it's different, too."

"That's why I come up here every night. It's why I live here. I'm surrounded by beauty without all the madness."

She turned to look at him, seeing already such a different man than the one she'd met four days ago. "What is the madness?"

"Cities. Noise. People." He hesitated. "Gossip."

Her brows pulled. "I don't understand."

Nikos's expression turned mocking. But she sensed he wasn't mocking her as much as himself. "You're better off not knowing," he said. "And there is no reason to know. You'll be leaving here in a couple months. It's not your problem."

Her frown deepened. Nikos was baffling. She was just beginning to realize he might be as scarred on the inside as he was on the outside, which raised the question—was he mentally and emotionally healthy enough to raise a child on his own?

Would he be a fit parent?

One more question she didn't have an answer for, but a question she knew she couldn't ignore. She did worry about him raising the child alone here. She worried that maybe he was a little too antisocial, worried that he was more isolated than was good for him.

She might not be able to change the terms of her agreement, but maybe she could change…him.

Or at the very least, help him prepare to become a father so that he'd be the best father possible. But to do that, it would mean spending more time with him, not less.

It would mean focusing on who he really was, and getting him to drop his guard…that rough mask…and seeing if he couldn't open up…become more emotionally available.

She had a little over three months until the baby was born. Couldn't she use this time to study and help him?

She just needed to formulate a treatment plan. She'd do the same thing here that she did in school: learn everything she could, soak up every bit of information, memorize every fact, every detail, and then review her case at the end of each day to monitor progress and make sure she hadn't overlooked anything.

Perhaps helping Nikos prepare for the birth would comfort her in June when it was time for her to go. Perhaps she'd feel more at ease with her decision.

Perhaps this was the missing piece.

Perhaps.

Georgia didn't sleep well. She woke when it was still dark, her room icy cold, but she was so hot she couldn't breathe. She kicked the covers back from her legs, her nightgown sticking to her damp skin. She shivered, chilled and pulled the covers back.

She'd had the old dream, although dream was an inaccurate description. It was more of a nightmare. Losing her family. Chasing through the trees for Savannah, trying to save her sister from the rebels, certain any minute she'd be killed, too. She was crying as she ran and then some-one was there with a huge machete and she was begging for her life because she was pregnant...

That was when she woke up.

She was having the old dreams again, but this time she was pregnant.

Maybe because she was pregnant.

Lying in bed, Georgia drew great gulps of air, feeling overwhelmed and suffocated by grief and despair.

This was not going how it was supposed to go. She was beginning to panic, and it was too late for that. She'd signed contracts and agreements and beyond the contracts and agreements, she was in med school, studying to be-come a doctor.

She didn't want to become a mother. She *couldn't* be-come a mother.

Georgia turned on her lamp and checked her watch. Four thirty in the morning. She wasn't going to be able to sleep again. She wondered if she could maybe go to the kitchen and make a pot of tea. The activity would be good. It'd distract her, help push the vividness of the dream away.

She pulled a thin cashmere sweater over her nightgown and then added a thicker button-down cardigan over that. After stepping into slippers, she headed for the kitchen on the ground floor.

She'd never been all the way inside the kitchen, and there was no microwave, so it was a bit of a game trying to find everything she needed. But at least the kettle was on the stove and she had a box of loose tea, a teapot and a tea strainer.

Georgia hovered over the stove as she waited for the kettle to boil, and her thoughts returned to the bad dream. And it was such a bad dream. But at least it was only a dream. What happened to her family wasn't.

For the past six months she'd told herself that the pregnancy wasn't a bad thing, either, because she was bringing life and light into the world.

She'd convinced herself that she was doing something good; she was giving Nikos Panos a gift. And, no, her mother and father wouldn't have approved, but they were gone. Her baby sister Charlie was gone. Her grandparents, who'd been visiting in Africa at the time of the assault, were gone, too. Georgia and Savannah were the only ones left, and in view of such darkness and tragedy, wasn't creating life a good thing?

Wasn't a new baby a miracle?

And since she was not going to ever be a mother, wasn't this a chance to do something good while providing for Savannah?

"Everything all right?" A deep voice spoke from the kitchen doorway.

Georgia jumped and turned around just as the kettle whistled. She startled again. Swearing—or it sounded as if he swore, she didn't know as it was a stream of muttered Greek—Nikos crossed the kitchen, pushed her away from the stove and turned off the burner.

"Sit down," he said sharply. "You're about to get burned."

"You scared me," she said, but she was happy to sit in one of the blue-painted chairs with the woven straw seats. She watched him use a pot holder to lift the copper kettle and fill her mug. Steam swirled up, shrouding his hand. "I had a bad dream, so I came here for tea. But I was trying to be quiet. I'm sorry to wake you up."

"I'm a light sleeper."

"Then I'm definitely sorry to wake you."

He flashed her a rare smile, and her heart did a strange, funny beat.

He was devastatingly attractive when he smiled. And

right now, watching him make her tea, his black hair thick and tousled, his long black lashes shadowing his cheek-bones, his full lips slightly curved, she felt her pulse drum faster.

She shouldn't want to know him. She shouldn't care at all, but she found him fascinating, and his scars just made her want to know more. They added an air of mystery. How did he get them? And why had he exiled himself to this rock of an island?

He'd virtually cut himself off from the world, and now he planned on raising his son here. Why?

"How did you get burned?"

He shot her a swift glance over his big shoulder, black brows flattening. He didn't look angry as much as sur-prised. "It's an old story. Not very interesting."

She didn't believe it for a minute. "I have a feeling it's very interesting."

"Not to me," he answered flatly, bringing the pot and cup to the table. "Do you drink it with milk or sugar?"

"Honey?"

He went to one of the painted cabinets and dug through bottles and jars but came up empty.

"Don't worry," she told him as he went to look in a bas-ket of jars and bottles next to the stove.

"It's here," he said, bringing a small ceramic bowl with a lid to the table. "Why do you have nightmares?"

So that was what they were doing. Tit for tat. "I've told you about losing my family in Africa."

"Not really. You just say you lost them. I'm interested in the details." And then his piercing dark eyes met hers. "I'd find it interesting."

"So if I tell you about my nightmares, you'll tell me about how you were burned?"

"If you tell me about your nightmares, I'll tell you about the burns…sometime, soon. Just not now."

"Why?"

"You have to trust me on that."

An interesting choice of words, she thought, stirring in the honey. *You have to trust me...*

The word *trust* had come up several times now.

"Okay," she said, not sure she was entirely comfortable with their agreement but thinking they had to start somewhere, building this trust, and she did want to trust him. She needed to trust him, otherwise how could she live with herself after she'd delivered the baby and returned to Atlanta? "But maybe you could tell me something else—"

"You're the one with the nightmares, not me."

She drew a deep breath. "The nightmares started a little over four years ago, after the assault. It happened when I was twenty, and in my final year at university. My sister Savannah had come to visit me, and we were looking at colleges together, so she wasn't at the mission when the attack happened. Thank God. She escaped."

Georgia looked down into her steaming tea, and for a long moment she battled the awful pain and tightness in her chest. The emotion was so intense. It made thinking, much less speaking, nearly impossible.

"They all died," she whispered. "My parents, my grandparents, my baby sister—Charlie. They all perished on the church grounds."

It was awful saying the words out loud, and the silence afterward was painful and heavy.

"What are the nightmares?" he asked after a moment.

She blinked hard, determined to stay calm. "I'm there and I'm supposed to save them. And I can't." She looked up at him. He was leaning against one of the kitchen counters, his arms braced against the countertop, and he looked so big, so sure of himself, and she envied him then. Envied his size and strength. Envied his fierceness and vitality.

The nightmares always made her feel so small and help-less. Vulnerable. She hated it, and she worked hard to keep from ever feeling weak.

"Is that what you dreamed tonight?"

"More or less."

"Tell me about tonight's dream."

She made a soft, rough sound. "It's too sad."

"Maybe talking will help."

She lifted her head and gave him a hard look. "Does talking about the accident that burned you ever help?"

"No."

She lifted her cup and sipped the tea. It was hot and al-most burned her tongue. Again tears started to sting her eyes. She blinked hard, determined not to cry.

"What's wrong?" he asked.

"Tea is too hot."

"That's not why you're upset."

Nikos was far too perceptive. "I just wish I hadn't told you about the attack—"

"If it's any consolation, you didn't say much. You didn't say how it happened. You didn't tell me who did it, or if they were ever caught."

"I hate discussing it."

"Is that why the information wasn't part of your donor file?"

"There's no reason for people to know. Savannah tends to be a bit more open about it. I can't stand talking about it. I get too angry."

"Angry...why?"

"My parents knew their work was dangerous. They knew what they were doing was risky, and it's one thing to put their own lives in jeopardy, but to put my sisters in danger? Charlie was just twelve. She shouldn't have been there. She should have been protected."

"And you said you weren't maternal."

Georgia's eyes felt hot and gritty, and impatiently she shook her head, regretting sharing. "I think I'll take my tea back to my room. If I'm lucky, I'll be able to fall back asleep." She rose and gathered her things, china cup and pot clinking as she accidentally knocked them together.

Nikos crossed the floor. He took the dishes from her, placed them on the table and then took her hands. "You're shaking."

"I miss them." And just like that tears filled her eyes. She turned her face away, trying to hide the tears.

"You loved them."

"So much."

She didn't know how it happened, didn't know what happened, but suddenly her face was tipped up and his head dipped and his lips covered hers.

It was impossible to know what his intentions were, impossible to know if the kiss had meant to comfort, because the moment his mouth touched hers, Georgia jolted as if she'd stumbled into a live wire. Sensation rushed through her in electric waves, making her shudder.

Nikos deepened the kiss, his lips parting hers, and she shuddered again at the pleasure of his tongue stroking the inside of her sensitive lower lip and then finding her upper lip.

It'd been ages since she'd kissed anyone. She couldn't even remember her last kiss, and Nikos was in total control, drawing her close, his hard body pressed to the length of her as lips and tongue made her melt.

She felt hot and explosive, her blood humming in her veins. She shivered as his hand moved beneath her long hair to cup her nape and then down her neck, stirring every nerve ending in her skin.

She couldn't remember ever feeling so much. Hunger gnawed at her, and her nipples ached, pebbled tight and pressed to his chest.

His tongue swept the inside of her mouth, teasing her, making her grow warmer, making her feel wet.

She shouldn't want this or like it. She should push him back, break free, and yet a small, scientific part of her mind was amazed.

This was unlike any kiss she'd ever known.

This was shockingly electric.

Chemistry.

His hands were on her waist, and then sliding up to cup her breasts, and she whimpered against his mouth. She felt wild with need, starved for sensation. Georgia pressed her chest against him, trying to assuage the ache.

And then just as fast as the kiss happened, it was over, with Nikos breaking it off and stepping back, muttering in Greek.

She'd bet a thousand dollars he was cursing again.

She looked up at him, and he looked grim as anything. Clearly he was regretting the kiss.

She fled. It was that or collapse in a puddle on the kitchen floor.

In her room, she locked the door and leaned against it, legs still shaking.

What just happened?

She'd never felt anything so consuming…pleasure and hunger and something else, something so intense that it continued to ripple through her in hot, dizzying waves.

Desire. Lust. Need.

Georgia exhaled slowly, trying to get control, needing to clear her head, and yet all she could feel was the pressure of Nikos's body against hers and the feel of his mouth… as well as his taste.

He tasted like heat and honey and licorice.

She'd never tasted anything like it. And God help her, she wanted more.

* * *

Nikos headed out at dawn to run his mountain. It was what he did when he wasn't calm, and couldn't think.

He put on running shoes and forced himself to run up his mountain to the top, where he'd put in the landing strip for his planes, and then at the top, he did wind sprints across the tarmac, letting the Cyclades northwesterly wind buffet him.

By the time he was finished, he was exhausted. The beast had been subjugated. He could return to the house without fearing for Georgia's safety.

He couldn't hurt her. He couldn't scare her. He must not disgust her with his sexual appetite.

That didn't mean he didn't still want her—he did—but he wouldn't break her door down to put his mouth on her taut nipple or kiss behind her knee until she opened her thighs for him.

As a boy he'd been fascinated by sex. As a young man he discovered he was quite good at it…pleasing women, making them sigh, making them come. He'd never imagined that you could like sex too much. It hadn't crossed his mind that he liked it too much, at least, not until he married Elsa and everything he thought about the world was wrong.

Correction, everything he thought about himself was wrong.

He'd thought in the beginning she was just inexperienced. He imagined she'd just need time to get used to married life, but it only got worse with time. She'd close her eyes when he kissed her and then turn her head away when he entered her; she'd hold her breath, waiting for his "animal side" to end.

Nikos had fallen in love with a woman who didn't love him, or even like him. It was a disaster from the start, and by the time the marriage was over, he loathed everything about himself.

And now Elsa's doppelgänger was living in his house, her belly round with his son, and he'd kissed her, and the kiss had been potent.

He wanted…

He wanted her.

But he couldn't have her. He couldn't. Even a monster like him could see why she was off-limits.

CHAPTER SEVEN

THE KISS CHANGED EVERYTHING.

Georgia had thought they'd formed a tentative friendship, but that was gone. Nikos avoided her like the plague—including skipping drinks at sunset—and even dinner for two nights after the kiss.

After two more days of punishing silence, Georgia went in search of him, which wasn't easy. He wasn't in his bedroom or the library. She circled the house, visiting each of the patios and terraces, as well as the pool. She returned to the house and checked all public rooms before going back to his bedroom. The staff said he was here; he hadn't left Kamari, which meant he was somewhere else on Kamari.

Georgia went out for a walk, determined to track him down. She finally found him on one of the more rugged paths that circled the mountain.

He'd been running, and his gray shirt clung to his damp chest. He was breathing hard as he drew to a stop on the gravel path. "What are you doing out here?"

She shrugged, not about to tell him that she'd been looking for him for almost an hour. "Getting some air."

"This isn't one of the garden paths. You shouldn't be this far from the villa."

"I'm less than a fifteen-minute walk from the house."

"But no one could hear you if you needed help. You need to stay close—"

"Stop it. I'm not going to do this with you."

He shoved black hair back from his brow. A ruddy flush colored his cheekbones, and his dark eyes sparked. "I didn't know you had an option."

She was fed up with his behavior. "I'm beginning to

understand why you required a surrogate to provide you with an heir. No one else would have your baby."

He wagged his finger in front of her face, nearly tapping her lips. "Is your mouth good for nothing but insults?"

She would have bitten his finger if she could. "Who do you think you are?"

"Your host and home for the next trimester." He leaned toward her, and his head dropped, his voice a deep rumble in her ear. "So I would try a bit harder to be cordial."

Heat radiated off him and she could smell the salt of his skin, and somehow on him, it was a good smell, but she didn't like his attitude and wasn't about to be scolded by him when he'd all but abandoned her for the past four days.

She shoved her hand against his chest to back him off but only managed to gain a couple of inches. "Please tell me that not all Greek men are as barbaric as you."

The corner of his mouth lifted. His eyes, with that curious ring of espresso, glowed hot. She wasn't sure what she saw there—frustration, yes—but there was something else, something powerful and seductive.

"I'm not asking you to be a submissive." His deep voice rumbled from his chest. "Just work with me."

"I'm trying! Can you not see that? It's why I'm here now. Why I went looking for you—" She broke off, realizing what she'd said.

He'd heard it, too, and he said nothing, content to just look at her, study her. Georgia felt the energy spark and grow. His dark eyes said things she knew he wouldn't say aloud. There was a chemistry between them that always simmered but had been teased to a flame now.

He wanted her. He found her attractive. And the attraction wasn't one-sided. She found him physically desirable, but this wasn't about love or long term. It was lust, plain and simple.

His word came to her—*carnal.*

She thought she was beginning to understand. He wanted her, and he'd bed her, and it would probably fulfill every sensual, sexual need, but that was all it would be. He wasn't going to want a relationship with her after the baby was born. And for that matter, she didn't want one, either. There was no future.

This…attraction…was potent, but it was only a distraction. It was just something that would pass the time.

But maybe that was a good thing.

Maybe that was the right thing.

Maybe she didn't want anything from him but this… the sparks, the heat.

From the moment she'd arrived there had been something raw and physical between them. They'd clashed over rules and she'd struggled for control, but she understood now that her struggle was resisting him.

But the simmering chemistry was about to boil over. Everything was catapulting forward, hot, hot and explosive.

"Carnal," she murmured, her mouth so dry she had to dampen her upper lip with the tip of her tongue.

"You're playing with fire now," he answered, his voice just as husky as hers.

A shiver raced through her. Excitement…anticipation. But she was nervous, too. She didn't want to take him on, wasn't trying to provoke him or challenge him. She just wanted to be closer to his heat and energy. It was electric. It made her heart race and her blood warm, and it felt so good to feel something strong and powerful, but the desire was also treacherous. It masked their true selves. It confused reason.

It confused her.

She had to remember why she was here. She had to remember who they were and what was happening… There were consequences for everything.

"You're not sure, are you?" he said, reaching for her, taking her by the arm and pulling her against him, into the circle of his arms.

She didn't provide much resistance. Truthfully she wanted him to kiss her again. Wanted to see if he still tasted of licorice and honey and him. And standing so close, his body pressed to hers, she felt the hard, taut muscles of his body and his warmth penetrating her clothes and she ached for more skin, direct heat. She longed to lift her top and peel his shirt up and let them touch, skin to skin. But if that happened, there would be no stopping them. She knew that.

Not because he'd force her, but because she'd beg him to touch her and taste her and take her.

She'd never wanted a man the way she wanted Nikos. It didn't make sense... There was no reason she should want him as much as she did. Maybe it was the pregnancy hormones. Maybe—

And then there was no more thought as he tipped her head up and kissed the corner of her mouth so lightly that her skin prickled and tingled all over. "You haven't answered me," he said, kissing the other corner, and then the bow-shaped upper lip. "Which makes me think you aren't sure this is a good idea."

"No," she answered, struggling to speak as pleasure streaked through her. The light kisses were maddening and delicious. She didn't want him to stop, but she couldn't lie to him, either. "Not sure at all."

He stroked her hair back from her face, his thumb caressing the high sweep of her cheekbone. "That's smart. Glad someone is thinking."

"Not clearly, though."

His dark eyes bored into her, the deep cocoa mesmerizing. "Which makes me think we should not be doing this. I will never take advantage of you."

"You're not."

"I'm not convinced." He stepped away. "We should go back."

She didn't know how he did that. Turn the heat on and off. She was still turned on. She couldn't quite find her off.

It made her want to hate him. Instead she silently walked next to him as they returned to the house.

Nikos left her at her door without a word, and she went inside and locked the door, not to keep him out but to keep herself in.

She practically threw herself onto the bed and grabbed a pillow to pull over her face to muffle the sound of her crying. She didn't even know why she was crying, but something inside her was cracking, changing, trying to break free.

Emotion. Control. Fear. Grief.

She was losing her mind. He was making her crazy. She couldn't remember any other man ever getting under her skin this way, and she wanted to think it was because he was arrogant and insufferable, but it wasn't that at all.

It wasn't his looks.

It wasn't the chemistry.

It was him.

The tough, fierce alpha who'd been terribly wounded somewhere along the way and was determined to live alone...apart...

It wasn't right. Nikos deserved better. And the baby deserved better, too. The baby deserved a family...a mother...

The baby...

Her hand went to the bump, and she stroked the curve of her belly, soothing him. *Poor baby...*

Her eyes burned all over again, stinging with fresh hot tears. She blinked and blinked again, but the tears were spilling.

What had she done?

* * *

She didn't go upstairs for drinks or dinner. She couldn't. She was still so upset, so heartsick.

Everything was coming undone.

She was coming undone.

She'd started feeling, and now she couldn't stop thinking, and it was overwhelming her reality.

She'd signed dozens of agreements and contracts. Everything had been completely binding. And she'd said she understood, over and over. She said she was prepared, that she was comfortable signing away her rights, comfortable because she was doing something good, she was helping someone become a father.

But now she knew who that father was, and she knew he had struggles and pain and he suffered...

At ten thirty a tray arrived at her door, even though she hadn't asked for anything.

She left it outside her door, not hungry. But she did go to the bathroom and shower and rinse her face. The shower didn't hide the puffiness at her eyes or how red they were from crying.

Georgia put on pajamas and crawled into bed with her books. She had to divert her attention or she'd never be able to sleep.

Half an hour later there was a pounding on her door. Only one person would pound on her door. Aware that he could very well force his way in, she opened the door to save him the trouble.

But opening the door to him was just opening herself to more heartache. Her heart did a free fall as she opened the door.

Just looking at him and her heart did another dizzying nosedive, the emotion wild and overwhelming.

He lifted a brow. "You look terrible," he said, his gaze sweeping over her.

She hated that he filled the narrow hall so well. Hated that he looked intimidating and sexy all at the same time in his wardrobe of black and black. "Thank you."

"You've been crying."

"Buckets." She gave herself permission to examine him as thoroughly as he looked at her, and she allowed her gaze to sweep slowly, leisurely taking him in from head to toe. "And why is it you wear black all the time? Are you a rebel or an outlaw?"

He ignored her jab. "You haven't eaten your dinner."

"I'm not hungry."

"Maybe not, but the baby is."

"No. The baby is fine."

His jaw tightened. "Don't do this."

Her own chin lifted a fraction. "I'm not doing anything but trying to survive here, Nikos. It isn't easy. You're not easy—"

"Never said I was."

"Thanks. That is really helpful."

He lifted the tray, carried it into her room and put it on the table. "Eat," he said, pointing to the chair before the tray.

She remained at the door, heart thudding. "I don't want to eat. I won't be able to eat."

His mouth compressed. His chest seemed to widen. "I'm not asking you. I'm telling you, Georgia."

"That's not going to help!"

"Then what will?"

"I don't know, but you playing the heavy won't. It'll just make me angrier."

"Can't have that." He pulled her against him, his arm wrapping securely around her waist, locking her against him. She shivered at the hard press of his body, his chest crushing her sensitive breasts, his corded thighs moving between hers.

"Stop fighting me, *gynaika mou*," he rasped, his mouth covering hers in a searing kiss. It was a kiss to punish, to establish dominance, to remind her he was the boss, the man, and this was his house. And Georgia knew all this, and felt all this, but it did nothing but flame the fire.

She'd been through far too much in her life to ever be a doormat. He wasn't going to take anything from her. She would take from him. Use him. She'd turn his aggression into pleasure.

Standing on tiptoe, she wrapped her arms around his neck, fingers dragging through his thick, long hair, welcoming the kiss, opening her mouth beneath the pressure of his.

He widened his stance and drew her even closer so that she could feel the urgent press of his erection through his trousers. His hands were on her hips, and he rubbed her against his shaft, the thick tip stroking her right at her core, finding her where she was so very sensitive.

She groaned deep in her throat, feverish.

As his tongue played with hers, stabbing into her mouth and then sucking on the tip of her tongue, she squirmed and rubbed herself on him, wanting the contact, craving closeness.

To burn like this…

To need like this…

She'd peel her skin off if she could…

"This is insane," he muttered as one of his hands reached up to cup her breasts and then captured the tight, aching nipple.

The pleasure was so intense her legs trembled. He worked the nipple once more, and she saw stars. She'd never felt anything like this, had never felt any sensation so intense. Her body had taken on a life of its own and she was shuddering as he cupped both breasts, thumbs teasing the peaks. She wasn't going to be able to stand much longer, wasn't going to be able to take much more...

And then his hand was at her waist, fingers stroking down to her hip and then trailing over her outer thigh. Every place he touched felt hot and tingly. The kiss was consuming, and yet Georgia was constantly aware of the caressing fingers on her hip bone and thigh, and then the press of his palm against her mound.

He worked the heel of his palm against her, applying just enough pressure to the sensitive nub to draw a muffled groan from her.

It felt good to be touched, and he knew how to touch her. He was making her melt on the inside, and she wanted more...more skin, more sensation, more pleasure.

She arched as his hand moved to her waistband, playing with the elastic band before easing it open. She felt the whoosh of cool air on her stomach and then the warmth of his hand on her skin.

Georgia closed her eyes as he slid his hand down across her belly, fingers light on her tummy, caressing to her hip bone, stroking there and setting fire to all the nerves everywhere.

She hadn't known her hip bone was sensitive, but clearly he knew something about women's bodies that she didn't. He was stroking down her hip and then beneath the curve of her buttock, cupping the cheek, sending shivers of pleasure everywhere. His touch was maddening, the caress stimulating not soothing. She ached between her thighs, her core clenching, and she pressed her breasts to his chest, rubbing the peaked tips across his, craving friction.

She wasn't wearing anything under her pajama pants and all she could think about was how much she liked the feel of his skin on hers, and the pressure of his hand, and the way his fingertips sent rivulets of pleasure racing through her. And while it was good, she wasn't satisfied. She wanted more…his hand between her thighs, his fingers on the sensitive nub.

But Nikos wasn't in a hurry. He seemed to enjoy the slow exploration, discovering who she was, and how she responded. She tried to be patient, tried to savor the feel of his warm palm sliding across her hip and thigh, drawing circles of fire wherever he touched, but she was melting on the inside and aching for relief.

His hand now was there, between her legs, tracing the seam of her, and then parting the soft folds. She began to shake, and she leaned against him for support, her legs no longer steady. Her thoughts were becoming incoherent as her body took over, focused on friction, sensation, satisfaction.

He stroked her, and she could feel how slick his fingers were just from touching her. "You are so wet," he growled, biting at her neck and then kissing where he'd just bit.

She was, too. She could feel the slippery tip of his finger stroke where she was so sensitive, and she groaned against his mouth. He did it again, this time drinking the cry of pleasure from her.

He caressed her until she dug her nails into his chest, and then he slid a finger inside her, carefully, gently, finding that spot that made sensation even more intense. He worked his hand, in and out, stroking her there, and she trembled against him. He seemed to know what she wanted before she even wanted it, drawing her in, making her ache and arch, yearning for that release that was just beyond her.

"Nikos," she sighed huskily, clinging to him.

He buried his finger deep, and she rocked on it, but the release wouldn't come. Hot, frustrated tears burned the backs of her eyes. She ached and wanted and needed.

"Nikos," she repeated, pleading for what she knew he could give her.

"Agapiméni," he murmured.

She didn't know what he said, she didn't care just then what the word meant, either. She only knew she needed him. She kissed him desperately, hands clasping his face, lips and mouth drawing the very air from his lungs. She kissed him as if he were her last breath on earth, and maybe he was, because suddenly his thumb was there, at her nub, stroking her.

Georgia was already wound so tight, nerves stretched to breaking, that just those couple of flicks of his thumb across her clit made her shatter, climaxing violently. The orgasm ricocheted through her, and she clung helplessly to him, her body shuddering with pleasure.

For a long minute after, she just leaned against him, listening to his heart, feeling the firm, even thud beneath her ear, struggling to catch her breath.

She didn't know why everything between them was so explosive, but the chemistry was beyond anything she'd ever felt, and just when she thought it couldn't be hotter, or more electric, he proved her wrong.

She slowly peeled away to look at him. Her pulse still raced and her body felt deliciously weak as she gazed up at Nikos, unable to think of a single thing to say.

He stared back at her, his eyes dark and focused and mysterious in the soft lighting of her bedroom. "Say it," he ground out tautly, adjusting the waist on her pajama pants and tugging her pajama top down.

She frowned a little, trying to figure out what he wanted from her. His expression was hard. White lines formed at his mouth. He looked almost…heartsick.

"Say what?" she whispered.

"How I disgust you, and how I forced you—"

"But you didn't, and you don't disgust me." She reached out to touch his chest, but he put a hand up, blocking her.

He made a hoarse sound and walked out, the door slamming loudly behind him.

Nikos avoided her the next day, and the day after.

Georgia told herself that she shouldn't have been surprised that he'd pulled away. It was the pattern now. But that didn't make the rejection any easier.

And the closer she and Nikos became, the more the distance hurt.

What had happened in her bedroom was intense—physically, emotionally—and part of her felt raw and rejected, but another part of her told her that Nikos was struggling even more.

She didn't know why intimacy was so difficult for him, but there was obviously an issue. He lived alone in the middle of the ocean, refusing to even visit the Greek mainland for medical appointments, insisting everyone come to him.

So, yes, she felt rejected, abandoned, but he was also wrestling with demons, and after two days of silence and distance, Georgia had had enough.

She found him on the top of the mountain, running sprints. He didn't see her there, not at first, and she watched him for almost five minutes, seeing him tear across the tarmac at full speed, running as if the devil himself was at his back.

Her heart ached. He was so tortured. His suffering baffled her.

What had happened? And why?

Obviously he blamed himself.

But this kind of self-abasement wasn't healthy. The way he handled stress worried her. Was this how he'd raise the baby? Would he handle problems as a father with the same punitive attitude?

She walked onto the tarmac, crossing the broad warm asphalt until she stood right where he was running.

Nikos dragged himself to an abrupt stop. He pulled out his earbuds, let them fall onto his shoulders. She could hear loud, pulsating rock music. It was the percussion-heavy, guitar-blazing, head-banging kind.

He was sweating profusely. His olive cheeks had a dark, dusky glow.

He looked past her, and then returned his focus to her. "How did you get here?"

"I walked."

"It's a long, steep climb."

"I took my time." She folded her arms over her chest, chilled by the wind. It was a blustery day. She'd been fine while walking, but standing still, she was cold.

Nikos just looked at her, distant, detached. There was no light or warmth in his eyes. She was reminded of the day she'd arrived. He was that Nikos Panos. Icy. Authoritative. Slightly hostile.

Her upper lip curled. It was smile or she'd cry. When she realized he wasn't going to speak, she did. "I'm worried about you, Nikos."

"There is no need to worry about me. I am not your concern."

"The nightmares were worse last night."

His head jerked up, and he gave her a sharp look. "Am I part of the nightmares?"

"You were last night, yes."

"What did I do?"

Her chest tightened. It hurt to breathe. "Nothing." She saw he didn't understand. "You did nothing, and that was the problem. The baby cried and cried, and you wouldn't hold him or pick him up and I couldn't get there and I couldn't help him—"

"So this wasn't about your family or you. This was about me and my son?"

Her heart did a painful double beat. "I'm worried about you, and how it will be when I leave. You can't just run away from things, Nikos. You have to face them—"

"I don't need the lecture, *gynaika*."

She'd found out from the cook what that word, *gynaika*, meant. It was woman. *I don't need the lecture, woman.*

She exhaled in a little puff of sound. He was positively medieval, and when he glowered at her—as he was now—scary as hell, but she couldn't back down. She had to do this, if not for his sake, then for the child they'd created.

"I am concerned. And you need to know that I'm troubled by what I see. You have moments where you are present and attentive, but then there are times like now, where you're so detached it's frightening. Nikos, this isn't the life I imagined for the baby." She saw his expression darken, the set of his mouth becoming grim. "It is one thing for you to retreat and detach if you have a wife and family, but you don't. You will be a single father, and you are so isolated here. The baby will be so isolated here. It's worrying."

"Worrying?" he repeated.

She heard the edge in his voice. Her pulse quickened in response. She had to be careful; she was walking on dangerous ground. "You must admit that is not going to be a conventional upbringing, living here on Kamari with just the two of you."

"I have staff."

"That is fine, then, if you are comfortable with them becoming extended family…grandparents, uncles, aunts—"

"They are staff."

She swallowed around the lump in her throat. "Don't you want your son to have more? Don't you want him to be loved and have family?"

"I will love him."

"Love is being present and accessible. But when confronted by something difficult you retreat…withdrawing for days. The child will suffer."

"You can't project what is between you and me onto him."

"Why not?"

"Because it will be different."

"Maybe. But maybe not. And because I know what I've seen here, and felt personally, I worry that when you need time alone, the child won't have enough love. I worry that he'll be…lonely. He should have others, Nikos, others in his world, others who will love him, too."

"I wasn't raised in a big, traditional family. My son will not miss anything."

She didn't say anything. What could she say?

His black eyebrows flattened. "You don't believe me."

She shrugged, trying to contain her frustration. "Children need community. They need to feel secure and loved—"

"I will do that."

"But what if something happens to you? Who will be there for him?"

"Nothing will happen to me."

"You don't know that! You're not God. You're mortal—"

"I think it's time you took a step back, Georgia. I am not sure why you are making my business yours. The child is mine, not yours." He stared at her, expression brooding. "Are you having second thoughts?"

She almost laughed. *Second thoughts? Oh, yes, second and third and fourth…*

She was consumed with regret. The guilt ached inside her. How could she have imagined she would be able to do this…conceive and carry a child and then just give him away?

"I carry your son," she said icily, "and I protect him with every breath I take."

"But he is *my* son," he repeated, "not yours, and therefore, not your concern. You waived your rights when you accepted payment. You waived those rights when you signed the fifty-some-page agreement. You waived those rights months ago, and you will never get them back."

Her fingers itched to slap him. He was hard and hateful, and his arrogant tone matched his arrogant expression.

It was all she could do to stand there and hold his gaze without crying or yelling. She stared up at him, staring hard to show she wasn't afraid and wouldn't be cowed. He needed to know that he wasn't a god. He wasn't the sun and the moon, the stars and the universe. He was just a man. A flawed man that had been broken and scarred along the way and survived by throwing his weight at the universe, thinking that he could control everything by being tough, cold, mean.

And she wouldn't shed one tear for someone who was determined to be tough and cold and mean.

She wouldn't feel anything for a man who was more beast than man. But at the same time, how could she hand a helpless newborn—so tender, so innocent—over to such a man?

"You're angry," he said shortly.

"Furious," she agreed, voice pitched low, vibrating with emotion. "And offended."

"Because I remind you of the facts? I force you to recognize the truth?"

"Because that kiss in my room, it changed you, and you in turn took something that was lovely and wonderful and made it ugly and sordid. You made me feel so good when you kissed me, and touched me, and then you pulled away and you've become hateful. You've become a monster... like the Minotaur in the labyrinth. You want to crush me now, but I won't let you. I might be a woman, and I might not have your size or muscles, but I am stronger than you. I will not break. And I will not let you break our son."

She turned around and started walking back the way she'd come, moving quickly, almost jogging back to the road, and then once on the road, she kept jogging, running, as if she could escape him, her and the truth.

She loved the baby.

The baby was hers...

She was grateful Nikos didn't chase after her. She would have had to run faster, and she didn't want to fall. She just wanted to get back to her room, to lock her door and hide.

But the moment she reached her room, she felt ill, cold and shaky and nauseous. She dashed into the bathroom, leaning over the toilet, stomach rolling, churning.

Her heart would break if she gave the baby up. Her heart would never be the same. How could she do this?

How could she hand him over and never look back?

It wasn't just because Nikos was detached and cold and hard. It actually had nothing to do with him, and everything to do with her. She loved the baby. She loved him and talked to him at night, and in her heart she talked to him throughout the day...

Tears streamed as she emptied her stomach.

Afterward, she clung weakly to the toilet, trying to catch her breath, trying to get her stomach to settle.

But her stomach wouldn't settle. The tears wouldn't stop. She'd made a pact with the devil. She'd sold her soul to make sure her sister would be financially taken care of, but the cost was too high.

The cost was unbearable.

She'd spent all this time telling herself it wasn't her baby, wasn't her son, but it was a lie.

He was hers.

And she loved him.

And it would break what was left of her heart if she left this island without him.

"This isn't good," Nikos said from the bathroom doorway, his deep, rough voice echoing in the small space.

She used her sleeve to dry her damp eyes. "Did you break the door down?" she asked hoarsely.

"I used the key."

"Thank you."

He disappeared from the bathroom and returned a minute later with a glass of water. He handed her the glass. "Rinse, spit and come talk to me in the living room."

She did as he suggested, and when she emerged he pointed to the couch.

"Sit," he said.

She wanted to tell him not to be bossy, but she didn't have the energy. Instead she sank onto the cushion and curled her legs up under her.

Nikos faced her, hands on his hips. "I don't like to see you this way. It's not good for—"

"The baby. I know." Her chin lifted. "I'm aware of that, and I don't want to stress him in any way."

Nikos's jaw tightened. "I was going to say *you*. It's not good for *you*."

She didn't know how to answer. She just looked at him, her heart so raw, her emotions wild.

"What is happening here?" he ground out. "I don't understand it."

"Understand what? That you kiss me and then run away...or that I tell you I'm scared and then you tell me it's none of my business?"

He muttered something beneath his breath. She couldn't make out the words, wasn't even sure if he was speaking English.

"What did you say?" she demanded.

"It's not important."

"I think it is. I think it's time you talked to me, Nikos. Not yell, not shame, not intimidate, not berate. Talk to me. Have a conversation."

"I'm not good at this."

"You'll get better with practice, and even if you don't want to do it for me, do it for your son's sake. He will need you to talk and listen. He will need you to not close down the moment you feel threatened—"

"I don't feel threatened!"

"You're terrified of emotion."

"That's not true."

"You run from intimacy like a little, scared schoolboy."

"What?"

"It's true. Conflict isn't going to kill you, Nikos. Having an uncomfortable conversation is just that—uncomfortable—but it's not the end. It doesn't mean we hate each other or won't still be friends—"

"Are we friends?" he interrupted, standing over her, black eyebrows flattened over dark, piercing eyes.

She had to think about the definition of the word for a moment. "Yes. At least, I think we should be. It's the only way to get through this. It's the only way I can possibly manage this last part...getting through to the end."

"So you do have misgivings now?"

"I don't know what kind of woman I would be not to feel conflicted. I feel him moving. He'll give a kick when I talk. When I go to bed, he gets active. It's like a game we play." Her throat ached, and the lump she'd been fighting grew. She couldn't say more. It would be impossible to say more, especially when the emotion was right there on the surface.

He dropped into a chair next to the couch and leaned forward, looking at her intently. "I have been making it harder for you, haven't I?"

"The whole thing is hard." She struggled to smile. "I don't know how we're going to get out of this in one piece."

"You make me nervous when you say that."

"And you make me nervous when I imagine you isolating a child from the world. Promise me you'll take him on trips and adventures…promise me you'll expose him to a life outside Kamari."

He searched her eyes. "I promise."

She blinked back tears. "Good."

"I will be a good father to him, too, Georgia. I will love him, and I will protect him—"

"Protect him from what, Nikos? From the world, or from you?"

He shifted, uneasy.

"You are only really, truly dangerous when you detach and disappear," she said. "I don't like your rough edges or your coldness when you're angry, but the distance…that feels like rejection. Abandonment. No one wants that."

"I pull away to keep from hurting you."

"You only hurt me when you pull away."

"I hurt you on the tarmac. I made you run away in tears."

"Because you'd pulled away! You and I had this incredible moment in my room and then you disappeared completely for days. It hurt. So tell me now, why do you do that after we're close? Why do you punish me?"

"I'm not punishing you. I'm punishing me." There was an edge in his voice, and tension washed off him in waves. "I should have had more control. I should have not taken advantage of you."

"You didn't take advantage of me. I took advantage of you. I wanted everything you did, and more."

Heat flared in his eyes, and she nodded. "I loved being close to you. You are so good at what you do…you're wow. Seriously, wow. You make me feel so good, but then you leave and I feel ashamed because I think my pleasure disgusts you—"

"No."

She lifted a brow. "Then why do you leave so quickly... and why did you avoid me after?"

"I wanted you. I wanted to carry you to the bed and strip your clothes off and—"

He broke off and dragged a hand over the bristles on his jaw.

She waited, but he wasn't going to say more. "Forgive me for being bold, but, Nikos, that sounds really good to me."

"What if I hurt you?"

"You mean, when you make love? Do you choke your partner...hit your partner...throw her around?"

"No!"

"Then what?"

"I am carnal."

"Is that a bad thing?" She didn't have that much experience. Sex was pretty much sex. She enjoyed it but hadn't had unusual experiences or anything particularly erotic. "Is that supposed to shock me?"

"I want you, *gynaika mou*. I want to be with you. I want to take you to my bed and keep you there for hours, touching you, tasting you, making you shatter with pleasure. But if we do these things, it will complicate us, and we are already very complicated—don't you think?"

Her pulse leaped in her veins. Her mouth had gone dry. "Yes."

"And so I try to stay away from you so that I don't kiss you again and put my hands under your clothes and touch you where I want to touch you, and feel you cry against my mouth as you come."

Her eyes widened. She swallowed hard. Her heart raced

now. She felt treacherously warm and wet between her thighs. "You like sex."

"I do," he said. "But I like you even more, and so I fight myself. I try to stay away, do the right thing."

"So that's why there is all this tension between us. You're avoiding me because you want me. And I'm lonely because I want to be with you—"

"You are not lonely for me."

"Oh, I am. I like you, Nikos. Even when you're awful."

"You can't like me. You barely know me."

She reached out, tugged on his sleeve. "Then let me get to know you."

"And how will that help either of us? We know how this will end—"

"Exactly. We know how this will end. There can be no confusion about the end, either. I'm not staying here in Greece. My world and life is in Atlanta. Yours is here. Neither of us is looking for a relationship. We're just trying to stay sane. Trying to make the best of an incredibly stressful situation."

"It doesn't have to be stressful, not if we stay on different sides of the villa."

She laughed low, but there was little humor in the sound. "Am I the only realist here?"

He looked at her for a moment, his gaze fixed on her mouth. She could feel his desire. Her own body hummed with need. She slipped her hand from his sleeve to the back of his wrist. His skin was firm and warm. She stroked the back of his hand, to his fingers, lacing her fingers with his. "I can't do this for three more months, Nikos," she whispered.

His jaw flexed. "We have to."

Her eyes burned, and her pulse raced. Everything in her felt stirred up. Her emotions were all over the place. She was physically attracted to him—dangerously attracted—

and yet he was right. He was everything she couldn't want. And perhaps he did know best. But at the same time she craved him, and his touch, and the pleasure he could give her. "I'm going crazy."

He pulled away, stood up and walked across the room. "We'll just try harder to stay out of each other's way."

The lump in her throat grew. "No! I'll lose my mind, Nikos. I'm already lonely. I already feel trapped. I'm not used to being cooped up. We need a break... A little stress relief would go a long way. Can we please go somewhere tomorrow? And if not tomorrow, then later this week?"

"Have you swum today yet? You didn't swim yesterday. Get in the pool. You'll feel better."

"I don't want to swim."

He shoved a hand through inky-black hair, pushing it back from his face. "Then go for a good walk—"

"Like I did today? Climb up the mountain to get a good hike in?" she interrupted fiercely. "Or perhaps I should try running. I only jogged today, but maybe tomorrow I could try a couple hundred wind sprints like you—"

"You don't need to run."

"Running won't hurt the baby."

"Walking is better, and you know it. Tomorrow it should be mild. Good weather—"

"No!" She jumped to her feet, hands clenched. "I've walked miles on your paths and they just go in circles. I've climbed this mountain. I've done everything I can do here on Kamari, and I need a change now. Please get me off this rock. Please let me see something new."

"You will be free to explore after the delivery—"

"That's three months away."

"I thought you had to study."

"I do study. For hours and hours every day, but I'm going stir-crazy. I need to get out...go see something, or go do something."

"There is nothing good happening in the outside world. You are safe here, so I prefer you to be here."

"If I am truly your guest, treat me like a guest and not a prisoner." She drew a short, raw breath as the possibility hit her. "Or am I prisoner?"

"What a silly question."

Her chest suddenly hurt, the air bottled in her lungs. He'd brought her to this island far from everything...

He said he didn't leave Kamari... He said there was no reason to leave Kamari. Her eyes widened. Was it possible she was his hostage? "Are you afraid I'll try to escape? Run away?"

"That's ridiculous. You're getting yourself worked up over nothing."

"Then why can't we go out for part of the day? You said you had a boat. Let's head to Amorgós, or even better, Santorini."

"No."

"Because I need to see people. I need to talk to someone. You've shut me out, and I understand why now. We have this—thing—between us and you're trying to resist it, and I understand that now. But I am lonely. I'm overwhelmed." Tears began to spill.

She struggled to wipe them away.

He swore in Greek and crossed to her side. "Don't cry," he said roughly. "Do not cry." He wiped her cheeks dry with the pads of his thumbs. "Don't cry," he said more softly, his lips near her ear. "Because you make me want to comfort you, and kiss you, but when I kiss you, *agapi mou*, I want you, and I'm afraid if I claim you, I'll never let you go."

CHAPTER EIGHT

THEY TOOK A motorboat to Amorgós two days later.

On the way, Nikos told her that there was a devastating earthquake on July 9, 1956, just north of Amorgós, between Amorgós and Santorini. The earthquake registered 7.8 on the Richter scale, and a second 7.2 earthquake followed thirteen minutes later. Intense aftershocks occurred for weeks, lasting through the summer.

Fifty-three people died on Santorini alone, and villages were destroyed on many islands. Quite a few people left the islands.

"I would think the earthquakes would have created a tsunami," she said.

He nodded. "Thirty-foot waves were reported all along the coast. And as difficult as this was, it's always been part of our history. The volcanic arc stretches from Methana—" He broke off, seeing she didn't know where that was. "Methana is a town on the eastern coast of the Peloponnese, built on a volcanic peninsula. And that volcanic arc extends from Nisyros Island in the west, to the coast of Turkey in the east. The arc is filled with dormant and active volcanic islands."

"There are some still active?"

"Absolutely. Milos, Santorini, Nisyros."

She of course had heard of Santorini but wasn't familiar with the other two. "Fascinating, as well as a little bit scary."

"Santorini always breaks my heart just a little bit," he said. "The Minoan culture was beautiful and sophisticated. And it was all wiped away. One day you should go there, visit the excavation of Akrotiri on Thera. There's a museum of found objects and some of the most stunning frescoes ever created. Many people believe that Akrotiri is the basis for Plato's story of Atlantis."

"I'd love to go there."

"It'd be a shame to miss. Perhaps in June you can travel for a while before returning to the US."

"You know I have the exam, so maybe *you* should take me there. Make it our next outing."

"We're not having more outings."

"Don't say that. Please. I still have three more months here. You can't bring me all the way to Greece and keep me on your rock."

"I don't go to Santorini."

"But you just said it's amazing."

"And it is. For others. But I don't go. I won't." He looked away from her, gaze fixed on the shadowy island ahead of them. "And before you push and push and spoil the day before it's even begun, I'll tell you—it's where my wife died. So I don't go there. Ever."

Georgia swallowed hard. It was the first time he'd brought up his wife, and there had been no tenderness in his voice, just ice. And grief.

They traveled the rest of the way in silence, but Georgia didn't mind. She welcomed the sun on her face and the wind tugging at her hair and she used the silence to think about what Nikos had told her...not about Greece but about his late wife.

She wanted to know more but knew that this wasn't the time. She didn't want to upset him or spoil their outing. It felt wonderful to be off Kamari, and she was excited about having a new experience. They might be traveling only twenty-some kilometers but it felt like an adventure, and she didn't care if they did nothing on Amorgós but walk around the little town and then up through the few houses before returning to the boat.

But as it turned out, there was plenty to do in the village of Katapola, Amorgós's biggest harbor. True, there weren't many shops, but Georgia just enjoyed exploring the town. Because everything was new to her, and it was her first real taste of a Greek village; she found it endlessly fascinating.

With Nikos at her side, she explored the pretty bay, dotted with fishing boats, white windmills and the traditional blue-and-white houses. Small cafés and taverns spilled onto the sidewalk facing the water, and on a side street they popped into a bakery so Georgia could admire all the different breads and pastries.

Georgia saw the woman behind the counter give Nikos a cold look, but he seemed not to notice, ordering one of each of the cookies so Georgia could try them all. She was about to ask him about the woman's odd behavior when Nikos opened the paper bag, drew out a cookie and popped it into her mouth. "Well?" he said. "Good?"

She wiped the crumbs from her lips and smiled. "Delicious," she said around the mouthful of almonds and honey and delicate flaky pastry.

"I thought we'd save them for lunch," he said, reaching into the bag and selecting one. "But they're far too tempting." He broke the slice of baklava in half, then handed her half.

She wasn't able to get her half into her mouth without making a mess.

Nikos watched her, amused. "You have honey all over your fingers."

"Not for long," she answered, grinning and then licking the tip of her sticky finger. She saw his dark eyes spark as she sucked on her finger, and suddenly her pulse quickened and she felt suspiciously breathless.

"I'd offer you a taste," she said, "but I'm not sure if that is appropriate."

"You love to torture me."

Her lips lifted. She smiled up into his eyes, wondering why she took such pleasure in provoking him. "Yes, I do."

"Why?"

"It's fun."

He groaned and took her arm, steering her from the bakery's front steps and away from the women entering the shop, their dark gazes all so curious. "It's not fun," he said, keeping her arm as they walked up the narrow street, the road cobbled. "I can barely keep my hands off of you as it is."

She flashed another smile up into his face. "So I've noticed."

"We are here to get away from all that."

"All that is you and me."

"You know what I mean."

"I do. But all that is us, together, and it goes wherever we go. It's not Kamari." There was laughter in her voice. "But it would be funny if the energy and magic was Kamari."

"Why would that be funny?"

"Because it's not a particularly romantic island. It's an arid rock."

"It's not supposed to be romantic. It's my home."

She laughed. "You sound so grumpy right now. What's wrong with you?"

He stopped walking to face her, his hands on her shoulders. "All I want to do is tear your clothes off of you and touch every inch of you, and you're making it almost impossible to forget how much I want you—"

"So don't."

"Georgia."

"Find us a room somewhere and make love to me. Maybe once it's out of your system, you'll feel much better."

"Stop it," he growled.

"What? I'm trying to help you."

"You're not helping. Because making love to you once won't get it out of my system. It won't satisfy me. It'll just make me hungry for more." His hands pressed into her shoulders. "If you wanted to help, you'd ask me the age of the church we passed on the corner. You'd want to know why there are so many windmills on Amorgós. You'd want to know how they make the whitewash on the stucco buildings."

"But I don't want to know about whitewash or the stucco. I want to know about *you*."

"Georgia." Her name was wrung from him, a low, hoarse groan of sound, before his head descended and he was kissing her, the kiss of a man drowning, dying.

There was so much heat and need in the kiss. His mouth was hard, and it slanted over hers, forcing her lips open. His tongue found hers, probing, seducing.

She shuddered and pressed herself to him, loving the feel of him—hard, muscular, all male.

An old woman passing by muttered a rebuke, and Nikos lifted his head, ending the kiss. His expression was rueful as he stepped back.

"What did she say?" Georgia asked, touching her lips, which felt tingly and sensitive.

"That we needed to get a room."

Georgia giggled. "I told you so."

"Hmph." Nikos took her arm again. "We're here to sightsee. We're going to sightsee. And you're going to enjoy every little church and interesting view, and in an hour or two we will have lunch, and after our lunch we will return to Kamari, where I'll lock you up for your own safekeeping."

Georgia just laughed again.

He glared down at her with mock fierceness. "I'm serious."

"I know you are, which just makes me like you all the more." She patted his arm. "When you're not growling and issuing orders, you're a very nice man and very good company."

"Don't soften me up."

"Too late." She flashed him another smile. "It's already happening. You, my dear Nikos, are putty in my hands."

"A *gross* exaggeration." But he was smiling and she felt her heart turn over because when he looked at her like that, she felt as if she'd somehow won the lottery.

Georgia was right, he thought later, as they sat in the back of the small taxi that he'd hired to take them all over the island. She'd gotten under his skin and was working some kind of magic on him, and God help him, he liked it. Liked her.

She made him feel things he didn't think he'd ever feel again, and he loved her smiles and her laughter and how she seemed to radiate sunshine even on a gray, windy day.

And while he enjoyed looking at her, he enjoyed talking with her even more. She was intelligent and witty and not afraid to stand up to him. Maybe he loved that most. She wasn't scared of him and didn't run away when he was impatient or frustrated. She held her own. She even pushed back, teaching him manners.

The corner of his mouth lifted.

She noticed. "You're smiling," she said, slipping her hand into his in the back of the taxi.

He glanced down at their hands and how she'd so naturally linked them. "What are you doing?"

"Pretending you're my boyfriend."

"Why?"

"It's fun."

"We're here to get distance."

"Kind of hard when we're smashed together in a car the size of a sardine can."

He grinned ruefully. She had a point. It was refreshing. She was refreshing. She made him feel young and hopeful, as if he were but a boy with his whole life ahead of him. "You enjoyed lunch, though?"

They'd explored the north end of the island during the morning, stopping at Tholaria and then Lagada, where they'd had a light meal, and were now heading south again, approaching the monastery outside of Chora, Amorgós's principal town.

"Very much so!"

He told her they were on the way to Hozoviotissa Monastery, and he mentioned that there was a dress code, but she was fine in her long, slim skirt and lace-trimmed peasant-style blouse, which she'd topped with a cropped delicate cashmere sweater that revealed her bump.

"In summer there are crowds," he added as the taxi pulled over to the side of the parking lot to let them out. "But we are lucky that it is relatively quiet today."

It was a long, steep climb up dazzling white steps. "Is it a museum now?" she asked as they began the climb to the church.

"No. It is still a monastery, but the monks are quite welcoming. They do have rules about visitors—no short skirts, bare midriffs or shorts on men—but we're dressed appropriately and I trust you know how to behave in a church, so we shouldn't have a problem."

They ended up spending an hour in the church and adjoining rooms. Nikos could tell from Georgia's rapt expression that she very much enjoyed the visit. The interior of the church was quite austere but there was a calm inside that was profoundly sacred.

Georgia knelt at one of the rails and prayed.

Nikos stood back, wanting to give her space, and yet also determined to keep an eye on her.

Later, as they left the church, she was quiet and somber. "What's wrong?" he asked.

"Nothing. I was just thinking of my family."

They were descending the stairs, and they were taking their time as the stairs down felt even steeper than the climb up. "Did you say a prayer for them?" he asked.

"Yes. I always do. But I also said a prayer for you."

"And what did you ask for?"

"Just that God will take care of you, and the baby." She drew a breath and blinked. "He will, too. You just have to trust him."

Nikos shot her a swift glance, but her expression was serene and she was focusing on the steps.

Halfway down she paused to glance back at the tall white face of the monastery built against the cliff. "I love places like that," she said. "They always remind me of my parents."

"Because they were missionaries?"

"They loved their faith and their work. And they loved each other. They were happy."

"But when they died, they left you and your sister penniless."

She shrugged. "Money doesn't make people happy. It just pays for things."

His brow furrowed. "And what will make you happy, *agapi mou*?"

"Doing something meaningful with my life."

"Like being a doctor?"

She nodded. "And loving my family. That will make me happy."

They reached the taxi, and Nikos opened the back passenger door for her, but Georgia hesitated. "Do we have to get back in the car?" she asked. "Can we just walk for a bit?"

"Chora is not far. We were going to visit the town and then head back to the harbor. Did you want to walk there?"

"How long would it take?"

"Fifteen minutes, maybe twenty."

"Let's do it. It feels good to stretch our legs. I think I was getting a little carsick on the way from Lagada."

Nikos spoke to the taxi driver, but the driver shook his head and pointed to his watch. Nikos shrugged and pulled out his wallet, handing over a number of bills.

"He had to take his mother to the doctor," Nikos explained. "But he said there are always drivers at the tavern. It shouldn't be a problem getting a ride back to Katapola."

"You're not worried about having to find a driver?"

"No. And I agree—it's good to be out. It's a nice day. You can feel spring in the air."

They set off, and Georgia tucked her hand through his arm. "I feel like I'm finally in Greece."

"I'm glad you're happy," he said, and he meant it.

"Let's stay overnight here. Let's not go back."

"We have to."

"Why? You're the boss. You make the rules."

He'd never seen her like this, not in the nearly two weeks she'd spent on Kamari. All day she'd seemed lighter...warmer and happier. She'd been thoughtful when they'd left the church, but she'd brightened again as they talked. "But we're only an hour from home," he said. "Too close not to go home."

"But that's what makes it fun. We're having a mini-holiday...and now we can make it a bigger adventure."

"And where would we stay?"

"I'm sure there are plenty of hotels—"

"It's off-season. Most would be closed—"

"I bet we can find one that's open."

"And if we did, you'd be disappointed. They are not going to be luxurious. The rooms would be small and simple. Quite Spartan compared to anything you'd find at a resort."

"Or like your house?" she teased.

"Or like my house," he agreed.

"You just don't want to stay."

"I prefer the comfort of my bed," he agreed. "And the privacy."

"But doesn't the routine ever get to you? Don't you want a change?"

"Clearly you do." But he wasn't annoyed; he was charmed. It was impossible not to be drawn to her with the sunlight making her glow and staining her cheeks pink.

He desired her more than he'd ever wanted any woman, and yet he didn't want to hurt her, break her.

And he couldn't.

She was pregnant. He couldn't take any risks with her, not just for his son's sake but for her sake.

She mattered. She mattered a great deal.

He'd thought she was cold when she'd arrived. Cold and beautiful. But he was wrong. She wasn't cold at all. She was intelligent and complex. There were so many layers to her. She could be fierce, as well as fiercely funny. It still amused him how she'd deliberately tried to provoke him outside the bakery. It'd been impossible to resist her when she'd smiled at him, her expression so warm, the light in her eyes teasing and sexy.

How could a man resist sunshine and honey?

And yet he couldn't have her.

But that didn't mean he didn't ache for her. He craved her touch and taste, her soft skin and ripe curves calling to him...

To fight the throb of his erection, he drew her attention to the ruins on the hill ahead of them. "The Venetian castle," he said.

"A Venetian castle in Greece?"

"There are dozens and dozens of them. Venice played a role in Greece's history for a thousand years. There are still Venetian fortresses and fortified villages scattered through the mainland and islands."

"I had no idea."

"All the windmills we saw today, those can be attributed to the Venetians, as well. The Venetians introduced the windmills for milling wheat—an essential form of income for hundreds of years—but the windmills fell out of use in the middle part of the twentieth century."

They were nearing the base of the hill with the castle. Georgia stared up at it, nose wrinkling. "It doesn't look like much," she said.

"There isn't much left," he agreed.

"We don't have to climb up there, do we?"

"It's dangerous. I wouldn't let you go up there even if you wanted to."

"Does that mean we have to go back to the harbor?"

"We can get a snack in Chora and then return."

"Or, can we see if we can find a hotel…?"

"Georgia."

"I've never stayed in a Greek hotel. I've never eaten in Greek restaurants."

"You did at lunch."

"We had olives and a salad and a delicious cheese-and-spinach thingy—"

"Spanakopita. Greek spinach pie."

"And I loved it, but I want more than just that little pie. I want to try more food and see more things. This is Greece."

"I know."

"It's exciting, Nikos. You're giving me a good memory to take home with me."

He knew she didn't mean back to Kamari, but back to Atlanta in June. His gut tightened. His chest felt heavy.

He didn't want to think of June, didn't want to think of her leaving.

For a long minute he said nothing, just stared out toward town with its brilliant white buildings and bold blue accents.

"We'll get two rooms," he said.

"We don't have to get two rooms," she answered. "Not if you're worrying about money."

"*Not* worrying about money." His lips compressed. "And we need two rooms. For your safety."

"I trust you."

"That's nice, but I don't trust myself."

She laughed.

Nikos found them rooms at a small hotel in the center of the town that advertised itself as Beautiful Villa. It was neither particularly beautiful nor luxurious, but it was neat and clean, and what Nikos said was typical of hotels on the smaller islands.

There was little to do after check-in as they had no luggage, and Nikos and Georgia dutifully inspected their individual rooms. Georgia was happy to note that they were close together. Not adjoining, but just a couple of doors down the narrow hallway from each other.

They left the hotel and walked to a nearby restaurant. It was quite early still, and the restaurant was deserted.

"They will think we are American tourists," he grumbled as they were seated by the window overlooking the town square.

"Well, I am an American tourist, and you can pretend to be a Greek tourist."

"No."

She grinned. "You don't want to be a tourist?"

"No."

Georgia couldn't stop smiling.

Nikos noticed. "What's happened to you? You are all giggles and laughs today."

"I'm having a good time." She reached across the table and captured his hand. "And I hope you are, too."

He attempted a scowl. "You've become overly affectionate, as well."

"I think somewhere in your hard little heart, you like it."

His jaw shifted, expression easing, and his dark eyes glinted. "Maybe just a little bit."

She squeezed his hand. "I thought so."

Over dinner of grilled lamb and fish and flavorful salads they talked about what they'd seen that day and the austere but mystical monastery. Georgia shared that she loved all the bright blue accents—the doors, the windows, the church cupolas—that turned simple Spartan villages into charming postcards.

"We know I've had a great time," Georgia said. "But have you?"

"I have, actually. I enjoyed the day."

"And you don't resent me for forcing you to have an adventure? I know how much you cherish your time on Kamari."

"And now I think you're trying to provoke me."

"Keeping it exciting," she said.

"Mmm. A rebel, aren't you?"

She mulled this over, then nodded. "I guess I am. No, I know I am. But in the end, it's what saved my life. Leaving my family, leaving Africa. If I hadn't insisted on returning to the States, I would have died with them. Savannah, too."

"You weren't worried about going to a big university in America?"

She shook her head. "I wanted a big American school

and wanted to do all the things I'd only read about. College football games, parties, movies, dates, fun."

"And was it fun?"

She nodded. "I loved it. So much. And I pushed Savannah to do the same. I told her she could always go back to Africa, but she owed herself the chance to be just a normal American girl for four years. Take four years, experience what everyone else your age experiences, and then decide what you want to do for the rest of your life." Georgia looked away and exhaled slowly, remembering the day she'd heard about the attack that took place at the church, at the end of a Sunday service. She'd heard it on the news, not even realizing that the missionaries killed were her own family until hours later when Savannah got ahold of her.

The day everything changed.

She changed.

Her inner rebel, that wild, free spirit, died the day her family did, and she matured overnight, becoming the person Savannah needed. Someone strong and fearless. Someone confident and focused. Georgia promised Savannah that everything would be okay. She promised her sister that they'd make it through, assuring the eighteen-year-old that there was no reason to worry about anything but graduating from high school, because Georgia would take care of the rest…and Georgia had.

She'd found an apartment for both of them to live in near the high school Savannah would attend. Georgia paid bills—which often meant using her credit card for everything, putting them deeper into debt—but she wouldn't tell Savannah or deny Savannah what was left of her adolescence.

"I became a donor because I thought it was the right thing to do," she said quietly, filling the silence. "I knew it would be hard, but it seemed to be the most practical way to provide. It'd pay the bills, and there were a lot. But surrogacy…that's something else."

"Tell me."

She shook her head. "Let's talk about something else. I'm getting sad. I don't want to be sad. This is supposed to be a holiday. Let's focus on happy things, okay?"

CHAPTER NINE

NIKOS PAID THE BILL, and they left the restaurant just as it began to fill up. The night was cool but not cold, and they wandered through Chora's narrow streets, getting glimpses of families relaxing at the end of the day. Men stood outside smoking together. Boys kicked a ball despite the shadows spilling into corners. Loud voices came from one house. A dog barked in another.

As they returned to the town center, heading for their hotel, they passed a couple with a stroller. Georgia and Nikos both looked down at the toddler, who was sitting up, taking in the world with wide, dark eyes as he contentedly sucked his thumb.

"I told you why I became a donor and a surrogate," Georgia said to Nikos as they stepped back to let the couple with the baby pass. "But why did you decide that this was the right way to start a family?"

For a moment she didn't think he was going to answer her, and then he leaned over and picked up a small coin he spotted next to the curb. He rubbed it between his fingers, cleaning it. "An American penny," he said, handing it to her.

She looked down at the penny he'd placed in her palm. Smiling, she chanted the rhyme, "Find a penny, pick it up and all day you'll have good luck."

He smiled faintly. "Should we call it a night?"

Georgia nodded, hiding her disappointment. She wasn't ready to go to bed, and she wanted to hear more about his marriage and why he'd chosen a surrogate, but she knew better than to push. He'd tell her if and when he was ready to talk. And if he didn't, well, she had to respect that, too.

Upstairs on the second floor, Georgia started to unlock her door. She was aware of Nikos behind her, and she kept hoping he'd invite himself in or suggest they have an after-dinner drink, even if her drink was just the bottle of mineral water next to the side of the bed.

"It wasn't a good relationship," Nikos said abruptly. "My marriage was strained from the start. Elsa was unhappy most of our marriage, and she thought a baby would fix things. I thought a baby would only make things worse."

Georgia slowly turned around, key forgotten. "So you refused to have a baby with her?"

"No." He folded his arms over his powerful chest. "But you have to sleep together to conceive. Elsa wouldn't let me come near her."

"Why not?" And then she shook her head. "You don't have to answer. I'm sorry that I ask so many questions."

"I'm happy to talk, but I think somewhere more private would be better. We'll go to my room. It has that little balcony. We can open the doors and get fresh air."

But once inside his room there was no getting past the bed without noticing there was a bed. Georgia suddenly felt shy, which was odd considering she was pregnant with this Greek tycoon's baby.

Nikos opened his bottle of water and filled the two glasses on the dresser. "Cheers," he said.

She lightly clinked the rim of her glass to his. "To a great day with my new friend, Nikos Panos."

He flashed her a lazy smile, a smile that didn't strike her as particularly platonic. "Sit here. It looks like the more comfortable chair." He in turn sprawled on the bed.

It wasn't a huge bed, either. It reminded her of a bed in children's rooms in America. She'd read that many of the European hotels were small, and so beds were small, too, but it didn't seem like a proper size for a man Nikos's size.

"Are we really friends?" Nikos said, studying her from beneath heavy lids with long black lashes.

"I think we should be. It'd make this attraction seem more logical."

"You feel it now, then?"

"The chemistry between us?"

He nodded.

"I felt it all day," she answered honestly. "I don't even have to look at you and I can feel you. And we can be laughing about something, but I know that if you touched me, or kissed me, I'd be done for. I'd just want more kisses."

"Hmm." He dragged his nails across the plain white coverlet on the bed. "You are nothing like her."

The words were spoken so softly Georgia wasn't even sure they were meant for her. It was on the tip of her tongue to ask him to explain, but then he looked at her, dark eyes piercing, and said, "She didn't like it when I touched her. She didn't want me to touch her. Elsa was uncomfortable making love...or at least, with the way I made love."

Carnal. Aggressive.

Georgia was beginning to understand. "She was the one who made you question yourself."

"It was no longer making love, but sex, and then the sex no longer felt consensual."

"What happened then?"

"We stopped sleeping together. She moved into her own room. I had mine. We lived like that for almost a year."

"Was it that way before you married?"

"We married very fast. I was respectful. We kissed and did things, but she wanted to wait until we married to have sexual intercourse, so we did."

"And then you married and she didn't want to do it?"

"I thought she needed time. I thought it was because it was all so new. But she said no—it was me. I was always angry and yelling and scaring her."

Georgia frowned. "Were you?"

"I became frustrated as time went on. And I may have yelled once or twice, but I was never cruel. I never said mean things to her. I never treated her badly. But I wouldn't release her from the marriage vow, and this I know now was the mistake. I should have let her go. I should have divorced her. It would have been better. In hindsight, I know it would have been the right way to go. But at the time I was young. Twenty-six, twenty-seven. I had a beautiful wife. I was proud of my wife. I was not going to just give up."

"Many people would think you were being a good husband, fighting for your marriage."

He shrugged. "I fought for it too long. I should have set my pride aside and let her go."

"Or had the baby?" Georgia looked at him, troubled. "Would that have helped?"

"I don't regret that decision. It was the right decision. I wanted a family. Elsa and I discussed children before we married, and she knew I wanted them, but I could not see raising a child as we were. I wanted to wait until our relationship improved. I hated how toxic it was. Wasn't healthy and it wouldn't have been healthy for a child. And then she was gone, and I wasn't just grieving the loss of my wife but the loss of the family we'd never have."

"Wouldn't it have been easier to just marry again? Start over?"

"I didn't want to marry again. I still don't. But I did want to be a father, and I'm looking forward to being a father."

"Marriage doesn't have to be bad," she said gently. "My parents had a good relationship and a solid marriage. They were still very much in love until the end."

"How do you know they were in love?"

Georgia closed her eyes, picturing them. It had been almost six years since she'd last seen them. Four years since they died. And yet it felt like forever.

"They were affectionate and warm," she said after a moment. "They were kind towards each other. My father was protective of my mom, but also respectful. My mother wasn't shy about telling us girls that we'd be lucky to find a man as good and kind and loving as my father. She adored him. And he made her laugh, which always fascinated me since Mother was quite serious at heart. She rarely laughed with us girls, but my father could make her giggle—" Georgia broke off, lost for a moment in time, seeing her mother at the kitchen stove, making dinner, and then turning as Father entered the kitchen, her mother's face lighting up.

"They were friends," she continued after a moment. "And obviously lovers, too, but their friendship and respect for each other was at the heart of their relationship, and that's what I've always wanted. Someone who would like me and respect me and treat me as an equal."

"It sounds so very American," Nikos said.

"The desire to be treated as an equal?"

"We don't think of marriage that way in Greece. It's not about equality but about fulfilling your role. To be a good husband. To be a good wife. It's easier to do that than asking, demanding, that men and women be equal."

"And your wife knew this was your viewpoint?" Georgia asked.

His broad shoulders shrugged. "We didn't talk enough about the important things. Elsa loved fashion and shopping, and she was eager to set up our home. My job was to work and provide—"

"You know that, or you expected she would?"

"She did not want to work. She wanted to be taken care of. And she knew I had the ability to take care of her."

"Was she beautiful?"

Nikos hesitated. "Yes."

"What did she look like?"

Another hesitation. "Tall, slender, blonde."

"Greek?"

"No. Scandinavian."

Like me, Georgia thought. But she couldn't just leave it at that. She had to ask, had to get his reaction. "Is that why you wanted an egg donor who was tall, slender, blonde?"

"Yes."

Georgia had to ponder this, as it struck her as odd that he'd want an egg donor similar to his wife and yet he wouldn't have a baby with her. He must have loved her very much, and it was on the tip of her tongue to ask him, but somehow she couldn't bring herself to put the question to him.

Or maybe it was because she didn't want to hear him say the words.

Elsa was gone and not here, so why introduce her? Why make her part of their night? Because this was their night... It was an escape...an adventure. Georgia was determined to protect the adventure.

As well as the romance.

Because there was something here between them, and it felt good. Special. And for tonight that was enough.

"I think we've talked about my marriage enough," Nikos said, sitting up. "Let's talk about something far more interesting. Let's talk about you."

"I'm not that interesting."

"I disagree." He was sitting on the edge of the bed now, his muscular legs extended in front of him. He gestured to her, indicating she was to come to him.

Georgia, who'd wanted to be close to him all day, suddenly felt a spike of panic. Her heart jumped, pulse quickening. It was one thing to anticipate seduction; it was another to be seduced.

He noticed her hesitation. "Have you come to your senses? Realized what a mistake this would be?" There was a hint of mockery in his voice, and yet tension rolled from him in waves.

She could feel his intensity from where she sat. He was suddenly very big and very male, humming with a primal energy that reminded her of a great cat on the prowl.

"You're making me a little nervous," she admitted.

"Why?"

"Because the kisses are always so good, but I've learned with you there's a price for such pleasure."

"We're not doing that anymore. I'm not doing that anymore. I'm not going to hide myself from you anymore. You will see me as I am. You will see more for who I am. Good. Bad. Ugly."

"Not bad, not ugly," she said.

"You don't know that yet."

"My gut is rarely wrong."

The corner of his mouth lifted and he gestured for her again. "Come, *gynaika mou*—I want to kiss."

"Just kiss?"

"I shall leave that up to you. You control this. You are in charge. If you just want to kiss, we kiss. If you want me to put my mouth on you, and make you come, I will. If you want my body filling you, then I will do that. I am yours to command. So come. Now. I am impatient for you."

She slowly stood, finding him utterly compelling and seductive. "But I thought I was in charge. I thought you are mine to command."

He leaned forward, caught her wrist, drew her to him. "After the first kiss. Let me kiss you properly, as I've wanted to kiss you all day, and then you shall be in charge."

He pulled her down between his legs, so that she was half kneeling at his feet. His hands clasped her face. His thumbs stroked her hot, flushed cheeks.

"So beautiful, my woman, *agapi mou*," he murmured, lowering his head to hers, his lips brushing hers.

The kiss was soft, almost sweet, and she leaned into it, kissing him back, and that was all it took for her lips to burn and her tummy to flip. She shivered as he deepened the kiss, parting her mouth to drink the air from her lips.

Hot, sharp darts of sensation rushed through her, making her head spin. She reached for him, wrapping her arms around his neck. He lifted her from the floor, kissing her as he stretched her on the bed next to him.

As he kissed her, his hand went to her waist and then slid up her rib cage to cup the softness of her breast.

She arched into his hand, groaning as he circled a nipple, tugging on it to make it even harder.

"You know my body too well already," she murmured as he dropped his head to kiss her nipple through her blouse and bra. His mouth was warm. His teeth found the tip, gently biting. She gasped.

"Too much?" he asked, lifting his head.

She stared up into his eyes, which were so beautiful and dark, and she shook her head, feeling wanton and yet good. "No. Not even."

"You want more?"

"I want everything."

"Perhaps we keep it to kissing for now, make sure you don't change your mind."

"I won't."

"We'll see," he said, lifting her long skirt and pushing the knit fabric over her knees. His mouth followed, his lips and tongue cool and then hot against her heated flesh. She was wearing small white satin-and-lace bikini briefs that sat low on her hips, below the curve of her bump, and his fingers brushed her, over the panties, over her mound and down between her legs where she was wet.

He stroked again, pushing her knees farther apart until

he had her open to him. Despite the white satin-and-lace panties, she felt so very naked and exposed. His hands were at her thighs, and he ran his palms down from her hips to her knees and then up again. Every place he touched burned. Every place he looked melted.

He was examining her, a possessive light in his eyes, his dark gaze burning and intent. Hungry.

Carnal.

Her heart thudded so hard it hurt to breathe, and she couldn't look anymore, overwhelmed by his intensity and the rawness of his desire.

She closed her eyes as his mouth touched the inside of her knee, and she sighed as his lips trailed up the inner thigh, kissing higher until he'd reached the edge of the lace. He stroked over the pantie and the fullness of her mound, and then slipped beneath the elastic, lightly tracing where she was wet and then sliding the wetness over her lips and clit.

His head dropped again, and he kissed where he touched, through the satin and then peeling the panties back, where she was pink and tender and glistening.

He did things with his tongue that made it impossible to breathe. He licked and stroked, lapped and sucked, and Georgia did not want it to end. She wasn't ready to come, but he'd wound her so tightly, her nerves stretched, her body tense with pleasure that when he slipped his fingers into her and then stroked up even as he flicked his tongue over her sensitive clit, she exploded, climaxing so hard she cried out, and grabbed for Nikos's shoulder, desperate to touch him, feel him, needing his strength to anchor her and keep her from blowing away.

"Amazing," she whispered as he stretched out next to her. She pressed herself to his side, still craving his warmth and determined to keep him with her. He'd said he wasn't going to walk away, but she wasn't sure, and she wasn't ready to let him go. "You are amazing," she added.

He held her against him, and she was content to lie in the circle of his arm until her heart stopped beating so wildly, but as she relaxed, she realized he was still dressed and she was somewhat in disarray and he'd given her pleasure but it wasn't what she'd hoped would happen.

"We need to get out of these clothes," she whispered, kissing his shoulder, lightly raking her nails over his chest.

He kissed the top of her head and then her temple and the side of her cheek, murmuring, "I think now might be a good time to get you back to your room."

"No. Can't go yet," she said, snuggling closer and lifting her face so that she could kiss him. She could taste herself on his lips and it reminded her of how giving he was, and how passionate, and how much she wanted to give him pleasure, too. "We haven't even begun."

"I don't want you to have regrets."

She wrapped her arms around his neck, welcoming the crush of her breasts to his chest and the feel of his thigh as it moved between her legs. "My only regret would be not making love to you."

"I have more scars."

"I've seen them. They're nothing."

"They're something."

"I think they're beautiful. They're part of you."

As he closed the balcony door and drew the curtains, she stripped off her clothes and then watched as he undressed.

Her eyes widened as his trousers fell and his shaft jutted up, long and thick and impressively erect. He turned off the lights, and she felt a little tremor of trepidation as he returned to bed, drawing the covers over them as the night was cool.

This had been her idea, but she was suddenly nervous.

Or maybe it was excited. It was hard to know when her pulse was beating double time and she felt as if she couldn't quite catch her breath.

Nikos pulled her against him, and she snuggled close, letting his powerful body warm hers, enjoying just being held. "Nervous?" he asked.

She nodded. "Just a little bit."

"We don't have to do anything."

"I know."

"Maybe you just sleep with me."

"Okay," she whispered, pressing even closer so that she could feel his hair-roughened chest scrape her breasts and his long legs intertwine with hers.

He was so warm, and he felt so big and protective. She couldn't remember when she last felt so safe.

Georgia put her hand to his chest and caressed over his rib cage, feeling the ridge of muscle beneath the firm, smooth skin. She knew his scars were higher up, on one shoulder, and along his neck. She stroked his back, savoring each hard, taut muscle, and then up higher, to the shoulder where she encountered thickened skin.

She felt him tense but didn't stop her exploration, caressing his broad shoulders and then down one thickly muscled arm.

"You have quite the hot bod," she whispered.

"The scars don't disgust you?"

"How could they? They are part of you."

"I think you will make a very good doctor."

She felt a pinch in her chest, a sharp reminder that this was all temporary, that she wasn't his for keeps, that they were just playing a game, staying busy, until June…

He must have felt the shift in her mood because he rolled her onto her back, stopping her exploration. "We don't have to do this."

He sounded somber, almost grim, and she ran her hands up and down his arms. "Oh, yes, we do."

"Why?"

"Because I want to be with you. I want to know what it's like being your woman."

For a split second Nikos couldn't breathe, the air trapped in his lungs, his chest seizing closed.

She wanted to know what it was like to be his woman. *His woman.*

There was fire in his eyes. A hot, gritty sting that echoed the burn in his chest.

He didn't think he'd ever have another woman. He didn't think he deserved a woman of his own.

"It's been a long time since I've been with anyone," he said gruffly. "Years."

"Not since Elsa?"

"Yes."

"Do you like being so celibate?"

"It is better than hurting anyone."

Her hands were on his chest, stroking over the muscle that covered his heart. "You won't hurt me."

"How can you be so sure?"

"Because you're a good man. An honest man. Not perfect but definitely likable."

He dropped his head, kissed her lips and then her jaw and then lower. She lifted her chin, giving him access to her neck and sighing with pleasure as he found sensitive nerves.

Her hands were caressing him as he kissed her, stroking his stomach, his hip, his thigh before brushing light fingertips over his throbbing erection.

He gritted his teeth, holding back a groan as she wrapped a hand around his shaft, discovering his weight and heat and length.

It was all he could do not to pump into her, to hold still while she explored him, cupping him, stroking, running her thumb over the head of his shaft, rubbing the drop of moisture over the broad tip.

"You are very impressive," she whispered.

"Let's see if I remember how to do this," he said, catching her hand to lift her arms above her head even as he settled his hips between her thighs.

She gave a deep, throaty sigh as he slowly eased into her.

"Does it hurt?" he asked, holding still.

"No. You feel so, so good."

The edge of his lips lifted. "That's encouraging, but I think I can make you feel much, much better."

And he did.

Georgia woke in the night, surprised for a moment to find an arm around her, holding her, and then she remembered where she was and what they'd done and how incredibly satisfying it'd been.

She needed to use the restroom, but she didn't want to wake Nikos. She lay there for several minutes trying to persuade herself that she didn't really have to go, but she did.

"What's wrong? Do you want to go back to your room?"

She turned to look at Nikos. She could just make out his face in the dark but couldn't read his expression. "I didn't mean to wake you."

"I haven't slept."

"What time is it?"

"Probably two thirty or three."

"Why can't you sleep?"

"I have you in my bed."

"And it's a small bed."

"It is a small bed, but that's not it. I've just enjoyed lying here, holding you. You feel good." He smoothed her long hair back from her face. "Why are you awake?"

"I think the little guy kicked me, reminded me I need to use the bathroom."

"I felt him move tonight."

"Did you?"

"Yes."

"What did you think?"

"It's amazing. A miracle." His voice dropped, deepening. "That you're a miracle."

Georgia sat up and reached for the bedside lamp and turned it on. She blinked at the brightness of the light, but she wanted it on to see Nikos's face. "I'm glad you finally were able to feel him move."

"It's rather incredible, isn't it?"

"Yes." He caught her hand, carried it to his mouth, pressing a kiss to her knuckles and then her palm. "Life changing."

CHAPTER TEN

THEY RETURNED TO KATAPOLA, the main harbor, for a late breakfast after checking out of the hotel.

Nikos had wanted to stay in Chora for the meal, but Georgia pleaded to return to Katapola so they could have their last meal on Amorgós be at one of those charming restaurants on the bay.

In town, Nikos let Georgia pick the restaurant, and she took the task seriously, studying the outside of each place before examining the posted menus before finally selecting a small outdoor café close to the boats.

It was clearly a place for locals—and by locals, it appeared the local men—but Nikos entered and took a table on the shaded patio, ignoring the curious glances from the patrons already seated at tables.

They knew who he was, she thought as he held her chair for her. Just as the woman in the bakery had seemed to recognize him yesterday. Just as the woman behind the counter hadn't been friendly, these men weren't welcoming, either.

"I know you studied the menu outside, but almost everything was for lunch. Greeks don't have a big breakfast. For some it's just a coffee and cigarette, not that I'd recommend that for you," he said. "For others, it might be some yogurt with almonds and honey, or maybe a slice of cheese pie or spinach pie."

"So what would you suggest?"

"What are you hungry for?"

"Do you think they have eggs?"

"I'm sure they could cook eggs for you. I will ask." He leaned back in his chair, looking carelessly at ease.

But Georgia wasn't relaxed. She could feel the stares of the men at the table in the corner. It wasn't comfortable. She shifted in her chair, trying to block them from view. "Have you been here before?"

"To this restaurant or the island?"

"Both."

"Not to the café, but to the island, yes."

She couldn't help glancing back over her shoulder, her gaze sweeping the corner table as well as the pair at an adjacent table. Not one of the men smiled or nodded.

"Kind of an interesting energy," she said.

"Very polite of you."

She focused on him. "So you're aware of the cold shoulder?"

"Absolutely. I'm not wanted here."

"Why?"

"They are uncomfortable with me here."

"Why?"

He didn't immediately answer, and then he shrugged, wearily. "They call me *teras. Thirio.*"

Georgia silently repeated the words. "What does it mean?"

"It's not important."

"Tell me, Nikos."

He sighed. "Monster." He hesitated. "Beast."

"What?" Her jaw dropped, shocked. *"Why?"*

He gestured to his face. "This."

"That's ridiculous. Those are burns. You were injured—"

"It bothers people here that I live and she does not."

"Were you at the wheel?"

"No. I wasn't even in the car."

"Then how can they blame you?"

"It's a small island. I live close by and yet I'm a stranger to them."

"I find it hard to believe that's why they call you such horrible things."

"I'm an eccentric."

"Yes, you are. But does that warrant such cruelty?"

"I don't know. I don't really care anymore. I just try to avoid this place. It's why I didn't want to come here. It's why I stay on Kamari. It's home."

His refuge.

Georgia swallowed hard, hating what he'd told her and yet also understanding his desire to be alone. To have his own space. To be free of ignorant people's hatefulness. "How do they even know about you and Elsa? Didn't you meet her in Athens?"

"No. She was here on Amorgós on holiday with girl-friends, visiting from Oslo. They'd booked a villa for a number of weeks during the summer and while here, she met a handsome young man, a local fisherman named Ambrose, and they fell in love. He proposed. She stayed. The wedding was planned. And then she met me."

"And she abandoned Ambrose for you."

"Yes."

"People took sides."

"Yes."

"And when she died in the accident, they blamed you."

The edge of his mouth curved, but it wasn't a smile. "You know the story already."

"It's horrible."

"I am, yes."

"No." She frowned at him. "You're not horrible. The story is horrible. And they are horrible, too, if they call you such terrible names. You are not a beast or a monster—"

"I don't blame them. She's gone and look at me."

"I see you. And I think you're beautiful." And then Georgia shocked everyone in the café by leaning across the table and kissing him on the lips. "Let's go back to Kamari," she whispered. "I'm tired of playing tourist."

It rained during the return trip to Kamari. The clouds had been gathering during the morning and by the time they boarded the boat at noon the sky was gray, the clouds ominously low.

"I am wishing I'd requested the yacht," Nikos said, taking Georgia's hand to steady her as she stepped into the low, sleek speedboat. "But maybe we'll beat the storm."

She'd had such a great day and a half on Amorgós, had loved her night with Nikos, enjoying every moment of their trip until they'd sat down in that café on the harbor.

Now it was hard to get the villagers' cold stares out of her head. Nikos's explanation didn't help, as she sensed there were pieces missing from the story. She wanted to ask more questions but didn't think this was the time. "I'm not worried about getting wet," she said, flashing him a quick smile. "It's just rain."

"You might feel different when we're flying at high speed across the water."

The storm broke while they were halfway between Amorgós and Kamari, and there were a few drops and then the skies just parted and the rain came down hard, and the wind whipped at them. The rain was cold and fell in heavy wet sheets, pelting them. On the speedboat there was nowhere to go, and so the rain drenched them, water streaming from Georgia's sweater when it could hold no more.

Nikos had offered his jacket when the first raindrops fell, but she'd refused. Now he simply overrode her protest and peeled off his coat, wrapping it around her slim shoulders and buttoning it over her chest.

"Nikos, I'm fine," she laughed, pushing wet hair back from her face.

"You're not. You're chilled through," he said. He reached out to touch her cheek with the backs of his fingers. "Your skin is cold."

"I'm not that cold."

"You'll get sick."

"We'll be back soon."

"Not soon enough," he said, drawing her into his arms and holding her securely against him. "Not taking chances."

"You never do," she answered as he shifted his hold, one of his arms circling her shoulders to keep her upright, while the other moved below the hem of his coat to clasp her waist.

She had been cold, but his body was warm, penetrating her damp clothes. She loved the feel of his hand on her waist, too. The intimacy of the touch wasn't lost on her. From the beginning Nikos had been protective, and on Amorgós he'd remained close, always watchful, always there to lend a hand as she stood up or navigated a steep set of stairs, making her feel safe, desired.

It had been a long time since anyone was there for *her*. She'd grown accustomed to taking care of herself, taking care of others, and it was a novelty to have Nikos want to care for her.

Nikos's hand at her waist was sliding down to her hip, and she sucked in air, eyes half closing, trying to ignore the faint shudder of pleasure.

"I knew you were freezing," he said, his mouth near her ear, his warm breath stirring her senses.

She wanted to tell him he didn't need to worry, that she wasn't cold, just sensitive, her body still humming with emotion and sensation from their night of lovemaking.

The speedboat hit a wave and lifted. Nikos's arm tightened around her, holding her steady.

Just then the baby kicked. Nikos's head dipped. "I felt that," he said.

Georgia's heart turned over. A lump filled her throat. She put her hand over his, trying to control the panic rolling through her.

How was this going to work?

How was she going to do this?

How was she going to just get on a plane and leave Nikos and the baby?

Back on Kamari, Nikos disappeared into his room to shower and change and work, and Georgia did the same, except after her hot shower she couldn't seem to settle down enough to focus on her books.

She sat on the couch and stared off into space, her attention drawn now and then to the window, where the rain drummed against the glass.

She had to study. The exam was important. Her future was important. Her goals hadn't changed. Her priorities were still the same. Weren't they?

But as the rain pounded on the roof and the wind howled outside, tugging at the old wood shutters, she found herself unable to see herself back in Atlanta.

She couldn't imagine returning to school as if none of this had ever happened.

Uneasy with the future, unable to answer any of the questions eating away at her, Georgia forced herself to read. She would study. She had to study. Right now preparing for the test was the only thing she could control.

That evening they met for drinks in the library since the rain hadn't let up. Nikos had laid a fire and the room was toasty warm.

He'd seated Georgia in one of the oversize wing chairs flanking the fire, and he took the other. The steady drumming of the rain was almost like music. Nikos couldn't remember when he last felt so comfortable.

He was content.

It had been a good trip to Amorgós. It had been time well spent.

Georgia was studying the fire, and he used the opportunity to study her.

She was so beautiful. So uniquely Georgia Nielsen. Fierce and frustrating, provocative and strong, and ultimately breathtakingly wonderful.

He remembered tracing her face in bed, lightly running his fingertip over her stunning face, following the elegant arc of her winged brows, and then down her straight fine nose, over the generous softness of her full lips.

"You are so incredibly pretty."

He didn't even realize he'd said the words aloud until she turned and looked at him, those lovely, tempting lips curving up in a smile.

"I have a feeling blue-eyed blondes are your type," she said, her voice warm with amusement.

He frowned. "Why did you say that?"

"You were very specific in your quest for a donor. Height, weight, hair color, eye color, ethnic makeup."

"I also wanted healthy, educated, intelligent—"

"Blonde." But her lips still curved. "But I'm not shocked. Men have types. Your type just happens to be slender blondes from Scandinavia."

"No, my type just happens to be you. The world is full of blondes, but there is only one you."

They ended up eating dinner in the library and then it was just a short walk to his room.

Georgia felt Nikos's impatience as he shut the door behind him, locking it.

"I've never been in here," she said, looking around. His room was simple with a large elegant bed, low handsome nightstands and a stunning glass chandelier overhead. "It looks Venetian," she said.

"It is. I have a weakness for Venetian design."

"Maybe you have some Venetian in your blood."

He reached for her, drawing her to him. "I know I have you in my blood." He lifted her face to his, kissing her lightly, his lips brushing over hers, teasing, making her sigh and arch into him.

"Kiss me," she urged, sliding a hand into the thick, glossy hair at his nape and giving it a little tug. "Make me feel good."

That was all it took for the simmering heat to ignite.

Nikos deepened the kiss, his lips parting hers even as his hand slid down her back, to the dip in her spine. He pressed her there, urging her closer. She loved the feel of his hand in the small of her back and the way his skin warmed hers from the inside out. She could feel his palm and the press of each finger, awakening nerves, making her spark and tingle.

His tongue teased hers. His hand slipped to her hip and then to the curve of her butt, holding her securely to him, letting her feel the thickness of his erection.

She rubbed herself against him, sighing as his shaft brushed her where she was sensitive. His fingers followed, cupping her there, between her thighs, and then stroking with expert fingers, sending a bolt of white-hot sensation right through her.

"Are you wet?" he murmured at her ear.

"Yes."

"How wet?"

"You could take me now, here, and I'd come like that."

"You are too easy." His teeth nipped at her neck; he stroked and pinched her breast. "We should make this a challenge. Not let you come—"

"No, not fair."

"Force you to wait, hold back."

"That will just torture me."

"But it will make the orgasm even better."

"I don't know that I'd survive it."

He laughed softly, his hands slipping beneath her blouse, circling her waist before sliding up her rib cage to cup her breasts. "I promise you'll survive. I would never let anything happen to you or hurt you."

"You have happened to me," she said, suddenly breathless as he peeled the lace cups from her breasts to rub his palms over her taut nipples. The pleasure was intense. He made her feel wild...desperate.

Before Nikos, she didn't think she'd ever really been touched before.

She didn't think she'd ever met a man who understood a woman's body the way he did. Nikos was a master of sensuality, an expert in seduction, and she wanted it all. She wanted everything he could give her, aware that this might be all they ever had, and it would have to be enough.

Her clothes seemed to fall away, and he drew back to look at her, his dark eyes hot and bright. He examined her from head to toe, ownership in his eyes, along with pride.

It felt good to be wanted...desired...claimed.

"You are so beautiful," he murmured, brushing a hand across one of her rosy-tipped breasts, her breasts so much fuller now that she was pregnant.

"I think you've been starved for attention here on Kamari," she said.

"I am starved for you," he answered.

"You had me not even twenty-four hours ago."

"That was a taste. I want a feast."

Her cheeks flushed. She burned.

He watched her face as he stroked her nipple again, tugging on the sensitive peak. She gasped at the ache he caused between her thighs. He was making her body so hot, making her wet.

He tugged on the nipple, rolling the tip between his fingers, the sensation sharp and intense, pleasure and pain, and Georgia sucked in air, head spinning, pulse pounding.

"I don't know that I can stand much longer," she whispered.

He swung her into his arms and carried her to the bed. His hands and mouth were everywhere, touching, kissing, stroking, licking.

Her eyes closed as she felt his lips close around her nipple, making her body hotter and wetter, and then he lazily traveled between her breasts, down over the curve of her belly. He kissed the point where her thigh and hip came together, waking every little nerve, before kissing her between the thighs, fingers sliding through soft folds, parting them to expose the nub.

The cool air against her was erotic, but there was nothing like his mouth on her, his tongue and lips covering her clit, sucking hard.

She shattered immediately. She couldn't help it. He was far too good, and she felt far too much.

"That's what I mean," he teased, moving behind her to hold her against him. "There is no challenge."

"Would it be better if I didn't come?"

"I would find a way to reach you."

"So confident."

He kissed the back of her neck, her shoulder. "I blame you. You have made me so."

And then he turned her on her side, and eased into her from behind. She was wet, and he was thick and hard. She sighed as he buried himself deeply within her before pulling back, nearly withdrawing.

She protested, and he laughed softly, teasing her for a moment before thrusting deep. He reached around to stroke her as he thrust in and out.

The pleasure built, nerves tightening, sensation focusing. She felt hot, and she was breathing harder, panting as each deep, hard thrust pushed her closer to an orgasm, but she fought it this time, not ready to give in, wanting to prolong the pleasure as long as she could.

Making love with Nikos was powerful…electric. The physical act somehow transformed her—them—into something beautiful and new, as if they weren't two separate people but one.

One body.

One heart.

And then she couldn't think about anything but the bright, intense sensation rippling through her, sweeping her into a fierce, brilliant, shattering climax. Her body exploded, and dozens of sparkly lights danced in her eyes, in her mind.

Heaven. It was heaven here on earth.

Georgia opened her eyes to discover Nikos was looking at her. "How long was I asleep?" she murmured.

"A half hour, maybe an hour."

"Did you sleep?"

"I just woke up."

She smiled sleepily. It felt so good to fall asleep in his arms and wake in his arms. She loved how beautiful and special he made her feel, as if she were the only woman in the world.

She could see in his eyes now that she was important to him. She could feel it in the way he touched her.

He always put her first, too. Her pleasure. Her comfort. Her release.

She liked that. Loved it. Maybe even loved him.

There, she'd thought it. Admitted it.

She was falling in love with him, and every time they made love, she fell that much harder.

She leaned toward him, brushed her lips across his.

"Are you just going to stare at me all night now?" she murmured.

"I was thinking about it."

She smiled slowly in response to his husky voice and lazy smile.

She loved the way he looked at her, focused on her. Loved the blistering heat in his eyes. Loved that he made her feel like she was a woman who could do anything.

"Okay," she said, nestling in and closing her eyes again. "You just do that."

Nikos watched her eyes close, and he knew by her breathing when she'd fallen back asleep.

He placed a careful kiss on the top of her head, overwhelmed by her in the best sort of way.

When he'd married Elsa he'd thought he knew what love was and how marriage would be. He'd imagined a relationship like his parents', traditional, practical.

Marriage to Elsa had instead been a constant source of conflict.

Her death had been a shock but not a total surprise. She'd threatened him so many times...threatened to hurt herself, hurt him, do something awful...

He'd been an only child. He hadn't been raised with sisters. He didn't have lots of cousins, never mind girl cousins. As he began dating, women were a bit of a mystery. Their emotions sometimes baffled him, but they also added a level of intrigue. He had girlfriends and lovers in his early twenties, but nothing in his experience had prepared him for Elsa.

He still wondered why Elsa married him. Was it his wealth? The family name? Did she think that one good-looking Greek could be interchangeable with another?

He would never know. He didn't want to know. He didn't even want to think of her anymore.

Her death, and the manner of that death, had nearly destroyed him. He was ready to put the ghosts of that past behind him, and he could with Georgia.

Georgia was strong where Elsa had been weak.

Georgia had fire and passion, courage and conviction.

Georgia's strength freed him. Her confidence and clear sense of self allowed him to be who he really was—a man, not a monster.

Her acceptance changed everything. Her acceptance made him hope for the life he didn't think he'd ever have.

A wife, children, a family.

He proposed at dinner the next night. He'd planned on making it special, wanting champagne and flowers, but it was still stormy and there weren't fresh flowers to bring in or champagne she could drink, so he just blurted the words.

"Marry me, *agapi mou*," he said, at the end of dinner, when it was just them at the table, with the flicker of candlelight.

She blinked at him, stunned.

He probably could have introduced the subject better, eased into it. He smiled at her bewildered expression. "Let's make this permanent," he said. "Stay here with me. Marry me—"

"What?"

"We are good together. We complement each other. I think we could be happy together."

She just stared at him, confusion in her eyes.

"I think this is a good solution," he added carefully, wishing he wasn't so pragmatic, wishing he was a man of romance. "We would be a family. You, me, our son."

She rose but didn't get far. Her eyes were wide. She looked almost afraid. "That wouldn't work, and you know it."

"Why wouldn't it work? You like me. I like you. We made a baby together. We should be a family."

Her eyes filled with tears. "It's not that simple."

"Of course it is."

"Nikos, I have school...exams...my residency. It will be years until I'm a doctor—"

"So wait until the baby is older and then go back to school."

"I can't do that."

"Why not?"

She shook her head and walked from the table, across the dining room floor. "I need some air," she said, heading for the terrace.

"It's raining, Georgia."

"Then I'll go to my room." She was hurrying to the hall, almost running to the stairs.

"Don't run," he commanded, cornering her in the stairwell. "Why are you so upset? You can say no. Just say no. There is no need for this. I would never force you, Georgia, to do anything."

Georgia shook her head, feeling cornered and confused.

She had been happy these past few days, happier than she could have imagined. And she didn't want to leave Nikos or the baby, but that didn't mean marriage was the answer.

"Georgia," Nikos said quietly, trying to get her to look at him.

She put a hand to his chest, torn between wanting to pull him close and push him away. "I have to finish school, Nikos. I have to finish what I started."

"But you won't have to work if you marry me. You can focus on our son. You can be a mother—"

"Nikos!" Her hand balled into a fist, and she pounded once on his chest. "I never wanted to be a mother! I wanted to be a doctor. And I still want to be a doctor. I want the life I planned."

He let her go.

In her room she curled up on her bed and grabbed a pillow, holding it tight to her chest.

That wasn't entirely true, what she'd just told him.

She did want to be a mother. She very much wanted to be part of her baby's life. But to give up her entire world back home? To give up her plans…her dreams?

To give up Savannah?

But, on the other hand, how could she give up Nikos and the baby?

There weren't tears for something like this. The questions and decisions were too huge and overwhelming.

And now Nikos thought she didn't want him, and didn't love their son…

How to fix this? What to do?

And then he was there, at the foot of her bed. She hadn't even heard him enter her room.

"Georgia."

"I'm not ready to talk."

"Okay. Don't talk. Just listen. I support you wanting to be a doctor. I think you should finish medical school."

"What?" She sat up.

"I think we can find a way to make this work. You, me, baby, medical school."

"How?"

"There are things called planes and hotels, houses and internet—"

"No internet on Kamari."

"Maybe it's worth the billion to put it in."

She laughed. "There has to be another answer. That's too much money."

"I am sure we can figure it out. If we're together."

"Yes." She left the bed, wrapped her arms around his

waist and kissed him. "Maybe we should go back to bed and talk about our options there."

"You have a most voracious appetite, *gynaika mou.*"

Her lips curved up. "Complaining about carnal activities, Nikos?"

He laughed, a deep, soft laugh that she could feel all the way through her. "Never." And then he was locking her bedroom door and taking her to bed with him.

CHAPTER ELEVEN

THE NEXT MONTH was without a doubt the happiest month Georgia had ever known. As the weeks slipped by with March turning into April, the rain disappeared and the sun shone longer, with the days warmer. It was by no means beach weather, but Georgia enjoyed changing from heavy sweaters to light wraps and sometimes no wrap at all if it was a particularly nice day.

The bougainvillea was bursting into bloom, too, and everywhere she looked there were huge clusters of hot pink and purple draped across doorways, over gates, up pristine white walls.

Georgia's heart felt lighter, and she didn't know if it was the fact that the sun always seemed to be shining and she was waking up to a blue sky over dazzling blue water, or if it just seemed brighter and sunnier because she was madly in love.

And she was madly in love.

She now also knew that she'd never been in love before. Nikos was her first true love, and after six weeks in Greece, she thought she could one day be happy here and maybe live here, but first she needed to finish school.

Nikos said they'd find a way to make it work. He said they just needed to take it a step at a time. One day at a time. It was good advice. The doctor had been there earlier in the week, and he'd said all was progressing well with the pregnancy. She was now in her thirty-second week. They discussed a birthing plan. Georgia said she'd be comfortable having the baby on Kamari as long as the doctor and the midwife were comfortable delivering there.

They discussed having a contingency plan, should there

be an emergency, and Georgia was relieved to know that a helicopter could get her to Athens quickly if needed.

All was good.

The baby was good. She gave him a little pat now.

To think he'd brought her and Nikos together. The baby had created love...a family...

Her little matchmaker.

She smiled and gave her bump another pat before leaving her couch where she'd been studying to walk across the room to put away the basket of clean clothes the housekeeper had brought up earlier.

On top of the folded clothes was a jeweled picture frame. It was a picture of her and Nikos, his arms around her, and they were smiling at the camera.

Georgia frowned, not remembering the picture. Or the clothes. Or anything about the oddly formal pose.

Maybe because that wasn't her.

It was another tall, slender blonde...

Georgia dropped the picture back onto the basket of laundry, horrified.

Elsa.

Nikos had just returned from a run and was stripping in his room to take a shower when the bedroom door crashed open. Georgia stood in the doorway, staring at him with huge eyes, her complexion ashen.

"What's wrong?" He moved quickly toward her, thinking that something must have happened to the baby. "Are you all right? What's wrong? What's happening? Do I need to alert the doctor?"

She just stared at him, looking as if she'd seen a ghost.

Nikos put his hands on her shoulders, gave her a slight shake. "I can't help you if you won't tell me what's happened!"

"Elsa," she choked.

He stiffened. His hands fell off her shoulders. "I don't understand. What are you saying?"

"She looked like me."

His jaw dropped as if he'd speak but he didn't. He couldn't. His mind was blank. "You don't want me," Georgia whispered. "You want *her*."

His brow creased. She was wrong, completely wrong. "That's not true."

"Then why does she look like me?" Georgia pulled a photo from her pocket. There were marks on the corners where it'd been worked into a frame. She thrust the photo at him, her hand trembling. "Look at her! Look. We're the same! We could be the same person."

Nikos took the photo, if only to keep her from shoving it at his face. He didn't even need to look at it again to know the one. He only had that one photo left. Elsa had destroyed the rest.

"Why didn't you just tell me?" Georgia whispered, tears shimmering in her eyes. "Why play this game with me? Why not just tell me the truth?"

"What truth?"

"That you're still in love with her, and that you miss her, and you wanted a baby that would be hers."

"But that's not how it is. That's not what this is."

"Really? Then what is it?"

But when he struggled to find the words, when he couldn't blurt out an easy answer, she shook her head and started to walk away. Nikos caught her arm, keeping her from going.

"Let me shower and dress. I just need a few minutes. And then I'll explain."

"I don't think you *can* explain, Nikos."

"You have to at least give me a chance." His dark eyes searched hers. "Meet me in the library in five minutes. Please?"

* * *

As Georgia waited for Nikos in the library, only one thought kept going through her head, over and over.

She'd been so happy.

She'd been the happiest she could remember...

This last month it had been almost impossible to study because she hadn't wanted to sit alone in her room, surrounded by books and notes. She wanted to be with Nikos. Her attention had wandered constantly, her thoughts drifting to him throughout the day. She'd wonder what he was doing, wonder if he was swimming, wonder what he was working on... It didn't matter what he was doing, either. She just wanted to be there, with him. Near him.

He'd never minded, either. He'd encouraged her to join him, be with him, sleep with him...

Now she knew why.

The library door opened and Nikos was there...tall, darkly handsome, overwhelming in every way.

He was dressed in all black, the way he usually dressed, and his expression was grim. But even then, her heart did a painful little jump and her eyes burned.

Her whole world turned inside out in just minutes. Everything she thought was true wasn't.

"Sit, Georgia, please."

His deep, commanding voice was so achingly familiar now, and yet she stiffened in protest. "I don't want to sit."

"It's a long, complicated story—"

"I prefer the shortest, simplest version possible, please." He gave her a long look. "You've already judged me."

"It's hard to ignore certain facts."

"Maybe there is no point, if you're not even going to give me a chance."

Her chin notched up. She wasn't sure she liked his mocking tone, but at least he wasn't begging. She didn't think she could handle that. "I don't know what you can say to

make it better. I don't know that there is anything that can
change this. I certainly know I can't compete with her—"

"You're not supposed to compete with her!"

"But that's who I am to you. I am her twin… It's as if
you've raised her from the dead." Georgia felt desperately
ill. Her stomach churned with acid and her throat burned,
and it was all she could do to keep from getting sick. "You
don't want me. You want *her.*"

"I don't. And for your information, you're nothing like
her."

"No?" Georgia glanced wildly about, looking for the
photo but realizing it was in Nikos's room. But she didn't
need to see the image to remember her shock as she looked
at a woman who could have been her twin. "Because she
looked an awful lot like me. And the resemblance cannot
be by chance."

"It's not," he said flatly.

"You wanted a baby with Elsa."

"No." Nikos muttered an oath and shrugged. "Yes."

Her heart thudded hard. Her stomach heaved. "And you
wanted to make love to Elsa, too."

"No."

"I don't believe you."

"You might look like her, Georgia, but you are nothing like her."

"And yet you loved her so much."

"I didn't—" He broke off, unable to deny it. "I wouldn't
have married her if I didn't love her, but what I had with
her is nothing like what we have."

"*Had.* What we *had.*" Her throat worked. Her eyes
burned. "There isn't anything for us anymore, Nikos.
There isn't an *us.* There is just you and her and all your
memories of her."

"Georgia, listen to me. You are not Elsa. You are not
twins. Yes, there is a strong resemblance but within min-

utes of you arriving here I knew you were nothing like her, and not just because your hair is lighter and your eyes have more gray in them, but because you are not her. She wasn't strong like you. She wasn't. Life was too hard for her. Love disappointed her—"

"Perhaps you disappointed her," she interrupted. *Just as you've disappointed me.*

His dark gaze hardened, shuttering. "I am sure I did." His voice had grown cold, too. "She took her life. She did it in front of me. Smashed the car into the side of the garage of our villa on Santorini. The car erupted into flames. I was able to reach in and pull her out just before the car exploded, but she was too badly injured. She died before the medics arrived."

"How do you know she meant to kill herself? How do you know it wasn't an accident?"

"She left me a note." His jaw thickened. "And every year I get a letter in the mail, from her, telling me how much she hates me and blaming me for ruining her life."

Georgia's eyes widened. "How is that possible?"

"I think it's just one letter that she wrote, but Ambrose, over on Amorgós, has made photocopies and he mails one to me every year on the anniversary of her death. The first couple years I made the mistake of opening the envelope and reading the message. Now I just throw them away."

"What does the letter say?"

"Something along the lines of, 'Nikos, you are a monster. I hate you with every fiber of my being. I hope you burn in hell.'"

"It doesn't!"

"It does."

"So why would you want this woman's baby? How could you want to be reminded of her on a daily basis?"

"I already think of her on a daily basis. I have the burns and scars from the fire. I have the letters that come without fail every August 16. But this baby isn't hers. The baby is mine. The future is mine. And she can't take that away from me…and I won't let her take you from me, either. I've lost too much to the past, Georgia. I'm not going to lose you."

This was so much to take in, so much to process. Georgia struggled to sort through her wildly tangled thoughts and emotions. "Nikos, I don't get this…I don't. And I don't want to hurt you, but it's just so…strange. It's not normal."

"Lots of people use donors. Surrogacy is quite common."

"No, I appreciate that you wanted to be a father and you found a way to do it on your own. I understand why you chose to go with a donor and surrogate, but why pick a donor that looks like *her*? Why not pick someone that makes you feel hopeful and optimistic? A donor that was the polar opposite of Elsa?"

"I did. I picked you."

"I don't understand."

"Georgia, you're nothing like her. Yes, you're blonde and have blue eyes, but that isn't the reason I selected you to be the donor. I picked you for you…your mind, your spirit, your inner strength, your desire to support your sister. In your application you wrote about growing up in Africa as a daughter of missionaries. You had goals. Ambition. Courage. And that was who I wanted to be my child's mother. I wanted a mother who had strength…who was a warrior. I wanted him to inherit your heart."

I wanted him to inherit your heart.

Her father used to say that to her mother. *I hope the girls inherit your heart.*

Georgia closed her eyes and held her breath, tears forming behind her tightly closed eyelids. It was too much, all of this. Too much emotion and too much pressure and too much shock and disappointment.

"Say something, Georgia," Nikos said quietly. "Talk to me, *agapi mou*."

She gave her head a shake. She couldn't talk. She didn't want to cry.

"You are my light in the dark—" His deep voice cracked, and he dropped his head, his fist to his mouth. "Please," he said roughly. "Please don't shut me out."

"I need to think. I need time." She couldn't look at him. Couldn't think much less feel when so close to him.

And then she was gone, heading back to her room.

Georgia left him in the library, escaping back to her room. She locked the door and then dragged a heavy chair in front of it for good measure. She didn't want Nikos to come in. She couldn't bear the thought of Nikos coming near her, not because she hated him—she could never hate him—but she needed to sort all this out and she wouldn't be clear, wouldn't be able to focus if he was near her.

This was important, too. This wasn't just about her feelings and her life, but this was Nikos's and the baby they'd conceived...not necessarily together, but still together.

Of all of it, the child was the most important.

He was innocent in all of this. He needed to be protected. Nikos was right. Georgia was tough. She was a warrior. She'd survive whatever happened next. But the baby would be helpless and vulnerable for years. The baby needed her to think and be smart. Logic was required right now, not emotion.

And logic told her that everything about her current situation was illogical. Irrational. She didn't belong here. She needed to go.

But the idea of leaving Nikos now took her breath away because she knew that if she left, she would never be back.

She didn't belong here. And the child?

She couldn't answer that one yet. Couldn't see that far

ahead. The only thing she knew with certainty was that she had to go.

And that knowledge devastated her.

For a moment she leaned against the door, her legs weak, her body trembling. Her heart felt as if it was cracking, shattering.

She closed her eyes, fighting for control. She drew a breath, and then another, cold...chilled to the bone.

Suddenly her stomach rose, heaved. She scrambled to the bathroom, fighting nausea the entire way. She prayed she wouldn't get sick. For long minutes she clung to the toilet, but eventually her stomach settled.

And then the tears fell.

She'd always prided herself on being smart, analytical, grounded, but she'd been played...duped. Completely duped.

Her heart squeezed hard, her chest so tight that she couldn't breathe. Pain filled her, pain and confusion, and yet one thing was brutally clear: she couldn't stay.

She had to leave. And she had to leave now.

Still shaking, she changed her clothes and then packed everything into her suitcases, jamming clothing swiftly into the suitcase and her books, laptop and loose ends into the smaller bag. And then she was done.

Nikos was no longer in the library. She found him outside on the terrace, the place they always met for drinks at sunset.

She steeled herself against all feeling as he turned to look at her. She willed herself to think of nothing, to be nothing, to want nothing. She was as she'd been before she arrived here—a single woman with a single purpose. The future. Providing for Savannah. Getting through the rest of medical school and her training.

She'd survive this.

She'd survived so much worse.

"Sit, *gynaika mou*. We need to talk," he said, his deep voice a hoarse rumble.

She ground her back molars, clamping down on all emotion, steeling herself against him. Everything in her still wanted him. He had such power over her. She'd found him nearly irresistible from the start. "No, Nikos. I'm not sitting or talking. I'm leaving." Her heart beat so hard it felt wild in her chest. "Goodbye."

He looked shocked. "You haven't even given us a chance—"

"Nikos, there isn't an us."

"Of course there is, and we've invested too much to just let this be the end. We need to talk. We can work through this. You know we can—"

"But I don't want to talk, and this isn't what I thought it was, either. You aren't who I thought you were."

For a long moment he said nothing. "How will you go? Where will you go?"

"Your boat will take me to Amorgós. I will sort out the rest from there."

"It's getting late—"

"It's not late. We have hours until sunset."

"An hour maybe."

"Plenty of time to reach the island if I leave now."

"You can't go like this."

"But I can, and I am." She backed up a step as he approached her. "And don't come any nearer. And definitely don't touch me. You will never touch me again. And you will never see me again."

"Georgia!"

She swallowed hard, chin lifting, eyes stinging, hot like acid, but there were no tears. She felt too cold and sick on the inside for tears. She was in shock. She would be in shock for a while. It was all too awful, all too much to take in.

"I'm going down to the dock. Have your man meet me there. He alone will take me—"

"I won't have it. I won't let you do this—"

"You don't have a choice. I'm not staying. I will swim to Amorgós if I have to and I'm happy to start now." Her gaze met his and held. "I'm not bluffing, either, Nikos."

His narrowed gaze swept her face. "I'm not saying you are."

"So call one of your staff—Eamon or Kappo or whomever is free—and have him drive me. But if your man isn't at the boat, at the dock, in five minutes, I will strip off my clothes and start swimming."

"You are being impulsive and dramatic."

"If you say so." She shrugged carelessly. "But I don't really care what you think. Fortunately, I'm a good swimmer, a very strong swimmer, and I've spent the past month swimming a mile or more every day here."

He made a deep, rough sound, and she didn't know if it was contempt or exasperation. "Amorgós is sixteen miles from here, not one, *gynaika mou.*"

"Good. It will give me time to calm down." She turned to walk away, then paused and glanced back at him. "And for your information, I am not your woman. I am merely your surrogate. Nothing more, nothing less. I will alert you when I give birth, and that is all you need to know for now."

And then she was gone, passing through the door, disappearing into the house, anxious to be gone, anxious to put distance between her and Nikos, the only man she'd ever truly loved.

CHAPTER TWELVE

GEORGIA ARRIVED ON Amorgós and found a little hotel in the harbor. It was a very small hotel, but it was open and had a room available and she was just happy to check in, put on her pajamas and go to bed.

Her plan was to just stay a night. In the morning she'd book a seat on the next ferry to Santorini. But as it turned out, in winter the ferry only traveled between Amorgós and Santorini twice a week and she'd missed it yesterday.

That meant she had two more nights until the next boat. Fortunately the owner of the hotel had no guests arriving and was happy for Georgia to stay the extra evenings.

During the day she sat in her room and studied. At night she would go to the tavern across the street and order something to go, and she'd eat her dinner in her room.

She didn't have much of an appetite, but she forced herself to eat for the baby's sake.

She tried not to let herself think of Nikos, which wasn't easy, since everything about Amorgós reminded her of him.

On her last night in town, as she paid for her dinner at the tavern, a handsome man in his late twenties approached and spoke to her in English.

"Is that his?" he asked, nodding at her belly.

Georgia stiffened. "Are you speaking to me?" she asked, voice frosty.

He ignored her chilly tone. "You look like her," he added. "Not exactly, but enough."

Georgia told herself not to engage. She was tired and hungry, and tomorrow she was leaving here for Santorini. "I'm sorry. I don't know what you're talking about."

"Somebody should have warned you when you were here last month. He is a bad man. *Teras.* Be careful."

Teras. She'd heard that word before. It was one of those derogatory terms the locals called Nikos. Monster, beast, something like that. "Who are you?"

"A friend of his late wife's." He paused a beat and then leaned forward to whisper. "He killed her, you know."

She arched a brow. "I don't know who you refer to. I think you have me confused with someone else."

"I'm not, and you know who I talk about. She was pregnant with Nikos Panos's child, too. But she'd rather kill herself, and the baby, then live with him." He gave her a dark, searching look. "You should know the truth as I'm sure he hasn't told you. Or maybe he has, and that's why you're here."

Georgia felt a wave of disgust and revulsion. "Are you the one that sends those letters every year to him? Ambierce... Ambrose?"

He straightened. "Ambrose. And so he has told you."

"Why do you do it? What is the point?"

"He was already rich. He had everything. He didn't need her. She was mine."

"If that was the case, then she shouldn't have married him." She tipped her head. "Good night."

Once back in her small room, Georgia locked her door and lay down on the bed and stared at the ceiling.

Was Elsa really pregnant at the time she died? Nikos hadn't mentioned that.

She placed her arm over her eyes to try to block out the pictures in her head, but it was difficult with Ambrose's words still ringing in her ears.

It was a good thing she was going to Santorini in the morning.

Pain woke Georgia up in the middle of the night, an ungodly cramping pain that made her fear the worst.

At thirty-three weeks the baby should be viable, but she wasn't home, and she wasn't near a major hospital.

She needed to get to a hospital. She needed help.

Struggling to get clothes on, she leaned against the wall during another sharp contraction, panting through the pain. She made it out into the hallway but couldn't take another step. The contractions were so close now. The baby was coming, and she feared the worst. She desperately needed help. She desperately needed Nikos.

Georgia opened her eyes. Bright lights shone into her eyes. There was a hum of voices and sound. A face wearing a surgical mask leaned over her, said something in Greek. Georgia had no idea what was said. She couldn't feel anything. She closed her eyes again.

The voices were just a murmur of sound, but it pulled her in. She struggled to follow. It was English. She should be able to understand. It was Nikos talking, but in English. He was talking to someone about the baby. She knew that someone, recognized the voice. A man…a lawyer, maybe? Mr. Laurent?

She tried to open her eyes to ask about the baby, but they wouldn't open. Or maybe they were open and she just couldn't see…

This time when she opened her eyes she could see. The room was dark except for a glow of light by the door. She wasn't alone, though.

Turning her head, she spotted Nikos in a chair, close to her side of the bed. He was awake, watching her intently, and his fierce expression made her heart turn over. "The baby?" she whispered.

"He's good. He's fine." Nikos's voice was rough. "You're the one we were all worried about."

"I want to see the baby."

"You will, soon. I think the doctors want to see you first."

"But he's really okay?"

"He's here a bit early, but otherwise, he's perfect."

She searched his face, trying to see what he wasn't telling her. She was certain there were things he was keeping to himself. "I heard you earlier speaking in English. I could have sworn you were talking to Mr. Laurent. Is he here?"

He hesitated for just a moment before nodding. "Yes."

"Why?"

"I wanted to make some changes to our agreement, and time was of the essence, so I flew him over. He arrived early this morning."

"What changes are you making to the contract?"

"We can discuss after the doctor has been in. He's been waiting to see you but I wouldn't let him wake you up. I can't believe how many times the nurses come in to check on you. It's impossible for you to get any rest here."

He sounded so indignant she almost smiled. "So tell me what's happening. Don't make me wait."

"I changed the documents. I gave you primary custody of our son."

She struggled to sit up. *"What?"*

"Shh, lie down, don't get excited." He gently pushed her back. "You are his mother, and a mother should have a voice and power and control."

"But why primary custody? Why not joint custody?"

"Mr. Laurent said the same thing." He hesitated. "But if I changed the agreement to joint custody, then I am forcing you to co-parent with me. I am forcing you to interact with me constantly, discussing everything from his holidays to his education to medical care. If we were on good terms, it would not be a problem, but if it is not good between us, it will be difficult and will create even more anger and resentment."

But she still didn't understand. "This isn't what you wanted, Nikos. This isn't what we were doing."

"He needs a mother. He needs *you*."

"And he needs a father, too. And you are his father."

"I intend to be his father. I intend to be in his life, but you will get to decide how we do this. It is my hope that you will feel empowered and secure—"

"Nikos, I never wanted to be a single mother!" she interrupted fiercely, tears filling her eyes. "This wasn't the plan!"

"I know you have school. Two more years of school. And then your residency—"

"And how am I going to do that now?"

"I will help."

"*You* will help?"

He nodded. "I am not walking away from you. I am not walking away from my son. I will provide financially, but I will also be there."

"How?"

He shrugged. "I have planes. I can fly to America, too."

"You are going to come to Atlanta?"

He shrugged. "If that is where my son is."

She opened her mouth, closed it, not at all certain what to say.

Nikos stood up. "I'm going to see if I can have them bring the baby to you. I think it's time you met your son."

Georgia was able to have a visit with her son—he was small, but, as Nikos said, he was perfect in every other way—before the nurses whisked him back to the neonatal unit, where they were keeping him warm and under close supervision.

Georgia had dozed off but was awake again, trying to sort out how she felt about everything.

So much had happened in such a short period of time

that it was difficult to separate her feelings from the facts, as well as the drama.

She'd missed Nikos when she'd been on Amorgós. And when she was in pain, and trouble, all she'd wanted was Nikos at her side.

She didn't want to raise a child on her own. She hadn't agreed to be a donor and surrogate to become a single mother. Nikos would be a good father, too. A very devoted father.

How could she take the baby to Atlanta and raise him there?

Even if Nikos agreed to go to Atlanta and share parenting responsibilities with her in America...how would that really work? And was that the right thing for any of them?

Georgia couldn't picture Nikos in Atlanta. It wasn't just because he was Greek—he was a man that needed his sea and his sky and his space. She couldn't imagine him in a city or even a suburb of Atlanta. But why was she worrying about what he needed? Why did she care?

Because she did care.

Because she loved him.

No matter how the baby had been conceived, it was their baby, and it was their responsibility to figure this out, sort it out.

She didn't know why Nikos had fallen in love with Elsa. She didn't know why Elsa wasn't happy with Nikos. She didn't know about Ambrose or any of it, and, to be honest, she didn't want to know.

She didn't want all the details. It wasn't her relationship, and she wasn't part of that bit of history. She had her own history and her own struggles and her own dreams.

She'd been happy with Nikos...blissfully happy during that month after they'd been to Amorgós, and before she'd found the photo on her laundry.

She'd wondered about the photo appearing on her folded

laundry, and she'd wondered if someone had put it there to hurt her, and then she'd dismissed the thought as irrational.

The door to her room opened, and a head appeared. "Is this Georgia Nielsen's room?"

Georgia's eyes widened, and she struggled to sit up again. "Savannah!"

Savannah grinned and closed the door behind her. "Up to having a visitor?"

"Oh, my God, yes. What are you doing here?"

Savannah rushed to her sister's side and hugged her fiercely. "I missed you!"

"I missed you, too." Georgia hugged her sister back, shocked and yet delighted. "When did you get here? How did you get here?"

Savannah sat down on the edge of the bed. "Nikos flew me over with Mr. Laurent. That Mr. Laurent is a cold fish, but Nikos is lovely." She took Georgia's hand, gave it a squeeze. "How are you feeling? Better?"

"I feel fine. A bit sore. But that will pass." She squeezed Savannah's fingers. "So you've met Nikos?"

"And the baby. He's delicious." She grinned. "Well, they're both delicious. I hope you're keeping him."

"The baby?"

"No. Nikos. I know you'll keep the baby. I didn't know how you were ever going to give him up. But Nikos. He strikes me as a little complicated, but you've always liked a good challenge."

"He's more than complicated. He's a disaster. He picked me to be the donor because I look like his dead wife."

"Yes, I've heard all that, and seen the photos. Mr. Laurent had some copies of the newspaper articles reporting her death—so tragic—but she didn't help herself any, getting pregnant with another man's baby and then trying to blackmail Nikos."

"Wait. What?" Georgia dragged herself into a more comfortable sitting position. "Slow down. Say that again."

"From what I gather, she never loved Nikos. She only married him for his money. She and her Greek boyfriend— he's a fisherman on a neighboring island—planned it from the beginning. She'd marry Nikos, accuse him of abuse or neglect and then divorce him and get a fat settlement that they could live on. But Nikos wouldn't divorce her, and then she revealed she was pregnant, and Nikos vowed to take care of her and the baby, but she didn't want to be with Nikos. She didn't want to raise a baby with Nikos. She didn't even want her Greek fisherman boyfriend. She just wanted to go home, back to Oslo." Savannah's shoulders lifted and fell. "It's crazy and sad and awful, and I can see why Nikos wanted to have a baby via a surrogate. I wouldn't want a relationship after that. Would you?"

"But I fell for him, and I thought he cared for me."

"I think he does. I am sure he does."

"What makes you think so?"

"He brought me here to see you." Savannah smiled at her. "And he gave you custody of the baby, too, which has to mean that he trusts you, and respects you…and believes in you."

Georgia exhaled slowly. "I have such a headache. I hurt. I'm not sure how I feel."

"About him?"

"I love him. I'm just not sure how this would work…or if we can even make it work."

"You don't have to know everything today, do you? Maybe you both just need to take it a day at a time until you know what you want to do. Personally I find snap decisions to be bad decisions." Savannah gave her hand another squeeze and then slid off the bed. "I'm going to go check on my nephew again, and see when they're going to be bringing him back to you. In the meantime, you've a big guy out in the hall, pacing like a caged tiger. Should I send him in, or let him keep pacing and scaring all the nurses and doctors?"

Georgia laughed. "Send him in. We don't need him frightening the hospital staff."

And then he was there in the doorway, watching her from across the room, a look in his dark eyes that she couldn't read and that made her chest squeeze tight.

"Why do you look at me like that?" she whispered, her mouth suddenly dry. She had to lick her bottom lip to keep it from sticking to her teeth.

"How am I looking at you?"

There was so much emotion in his eyes, so much worry, too. His worry made her heart ache and turn over.

"You look at me as if I'm something wonderful," she whispered.

He made a rough sound in the back of his throat. "Because you are."

He crossed the room, approached the bed. Leaning over her, he gently untangled a long golden strand of hair from her cheek, smoothing the silken strand back to lie with the others. "And I look at you with wonder because when you left me last week, I thought I'd lost you forever, and yet here you are, and here our son is, and all I know is that I cannot bear to lose either of you, but at the same time, I refuse to trap you with me. I refuse to use our son to keep you at my side."

"Is that why you gave me custody? You didn't want me to feel pressured into staying with you?"

"I want nothing more than to live together and raise him together, but it must be right for you. I want what is best for you and our child. I give you control so that you know you are not a vessel or a surrogate. You are not my captive, either." His lips twisted. "You are a beautiful, strong, intelligent woman, and I love you with all my heart."

She searched his eyes. "This could backfire on you, Nikos. You could lose everything."

"My attorney said the same thing. But I will never be happy if you aren't happy, and you have much to achieve in this world, big things ahead of you. I will not stand in your way. If anything, I'd like to support you and help you reach those dreams."

"Even if it means we live in Atlanta?"

"I am planning on living in Atlanta. I've even been looking at real estate. A big house, lots of land around us, plenty of space."

"That will be very expensive in Atlanta."

He shrugged. "I am sure I can afford it."

"You really mean this? You'd go to Atlanta…you'd help me raise the baby there while I finish school?"

"Of course. You are my woman, my love, and hopefully one day, *yineka mou*, my wife."

Her head was spinning. She couldn't quite grasp everything he was saying. "You really have looked at real estate in Atlanta?"

"Yes. I found a couple places that look interesting. I thought we could go have a look when the baby is cleared for travel. Might be a couple weeks."

He *was* serious. This was crazy but wonderful. It hadn't ever crossed her mind that he'd really be willing to go with her to Georgia. It would help things immensely if they were all together. The baby could have them both…

"I think this is a very interesting plan," she said carefully. "But it's also a lot to take in. You, me, the baby—" She broke off, frowned. "And do we even want to talk about a name for him? I think at some point he might object to just being called the baby."

Nikos laughed, a deep, rumbling laugh that filled the room and made Georgia smile. She'd never heard him laugh, not like that, and she thought it had to be the very best sound in the world.

Tears started to fill her eyes, and then she wasn't smiling but crying, and Nikos was holding her.

"What's wrong, *agapi mou*—what's happened?" He soothed her, stroking the back of her head, trying his best to comfort her.

"Everything is happening, and these hormones don't help," she choked out.

"It's okay. Cry. It might help make you feel better."

"I doubt it." She sniffed, wiping her cheeks dry, struggling to get control. "So what happens to us, Nikos, if we go to Atlanta together? How will this work?"

"What are you asking?"

"I care for you, Nikos, so very much, but there are things we don't know about each other, and things we need to discover. Can we slow things down a little? Back up a bit so that we are just dating and we can use the time in Atlanta to figure out if we are good together…happy together?"

"You're breaking off the engagement?"

"Well, I never had a ring…"

He smiled. "This is true. We couldn't possibly have been engaged then. So we're back to square one. Starting over."

"Not totally starting over. We do have a son."

He leaned over the bed, kissed her, then kissed her again. "Speaking of our son, I agree with you that it's time to consider names."

"Can you go get him, see if he can join us? I have a feeling he'd like to be present for something this significant."

EPILOGUE

GEORGIA SHOULD HAVE been stressed. She had a four-month-old baby who was still nursing around the clock and she was waiting on the results from the grueling exams she'd taken three weeks ago. She should be getting the results next Wednesday, but she wasn't worried.

If anything, she was calm, and incredibly, ridiculously happy.

She loved Alek Panos so much that it made her heart ache, but what gave her even greater joy was seeing Nikos and Alek together. No one could soothe Alek like his father. Nikos had spent many a night pacing the nursery or rocking him in the big chair in the corner of their master bedroom.

Alek had been so small, being born early, but he was quickly putting on weight and was catching up with the crucial milestones.

Tomorrow they were baptizing him and they were hosting a small dinner at their house to celebrate afterward. Savannah would be there, of course, as she was Alek's godmother, and they'd invited a few other people to join them, mostly Georgia's friends from medical school, along with Mr. Laurent and his wife.

Who would have ever imagined that Mr. Laurent would become their friend, and even a surrogate grandfather to Alek?

Life was good, Georgia thought, lightly patting Alek's back. He'd been nursing and had fallen asleep on the job. She smiled faintly, savoring the feel of him on her chest. He was so warm and sweet. She loved him to pieces…

loved him so much she wondered now why she'd thought she wouldn't be a good mother.

The door to the nursery opened, and Nikos entered.

Her heart gave a little jump as he smiled at her. She grinned back. It was impossible not to smile when she saw him. He made her so happy. He was her other half.

"Hey," she whispered.

"He's out?" Nikos asked.

She nodded. "He did pretty good. Hoping he got enough to get him through a good long nap."

"Should I put him back in his crib?"

"I'm okay holding him. It feels good just to hold him. He's getting bigger every day."

"That's good. He's healthy."

"I'm so grateful. He's a blessing." She dropped a light kiss on his tender head. "Everything okay?"

Nikos took a seat on the ottoman next to her feet. "Just a few days until you get your test results," he said.

"I know."

"Nervous?"

She thought about it. "No. I'm actually pretty Zen."

"Lots of people take them again."

"I'm not worried, either way. Whatever will be, will be." Her gaze met his and held. "I'm happy, Nikos, really happy. I love Alek. I love us. This is everything I ever wanted. Doing well on the test would just be icing on the cake."

"If you do well, you'll have many options. You'll be able to complete your training at any number of hospitals."

She nodded. "I've looked into different programs, and there are places that look good, but, Nikos, I think my first choice would be returning to Greece."

"Is there a program in Athens?"

She hesitated. "I think I'd just like to go home to Kamari… I think I'd like to just be a mother for the next couple of years and then we can talk about the rest, when we're ready. When I'm ready."

She thought he'd be excited about her decision. She thought he'd be happy for her, but Nikos wasn't smiling. He looked troubled...worried. "Can you take time off and return? Won't that set you back?"

"I can always return to school when he's older. But I'll never get these years back. And not just with him, but with you. Nikos, *agapo mou*, I adore you."

Emotion darkened his beautiful eyes. "You speak Greek now, too?"

"I've learned the most important phrases." She smiled and reached for him, drawing his face to hers. She kissed him once, and then again, whispering, *"S'agapo." I love you.*

He kissed her back, careful not to bump Alek. "My brilliant Georgia," he murmured. "You take my breath away."

He was still kissing her when the door opened and a cough sounded in the doorway. It was Savannah, and she was smiling. "Maybe you two need to get a room," she said in a stage whisper. "In fact, I know you need to get a room. Don't worry about a thing. I've got the baby."

They didn't need persuading.

Georgia carefully put Alek in his crib, and Nikos took her hand, leading her from the nursery to their master suite at the end of the hall.

It was a huge house, a Tudor-style mansion on a couple of acres in Atlanta's oldest and best neighborhood, but that wasn't why Georgia liked it. She liked it because they had the biggest bed she'd ever seen, giving her and Nikos lots of room to play and sleep.

Inside their room he slid the lock shut and drew her into his arms, kissing her with a hunger that let her know just how much he wanted her and needed her.

His hands were on her waist and then curving over her hips, pulling her close against his erection.

Georgia shivered with pleasure. "Thank goodness for sisters who love to babysit," she said. "I love her timing."

He nibbled at her neck and kissed the hollow beneath her ear. "So do I. She arrived right on schedule."

Georgia lifted her head. "What schedule?"

He smiled, kissed her. "Come see." Taking her by the hand, he led her to the table in front of the huge bow-shaped window, where there was champagne in an ornate silver bucket. Crystal flutes stood next to the bucket and there were silver trays of food, gorgeous-looking food, along with enormous vases of red roses.

Her eyes widened as she looked back at him. "Nikos… is this what I think it is?"

"Flowers and champagne? Yes. Yes, it is."

She giggled and hugged him. "Seriously. What's going on?"

"We're celebrating you. Because I love you. And you are the most beautiful and amazing woman in the world."

She swallowed hard as her eyes began to prickle and burn.

"I love you, Georgia. I will always love you." He drew a black leather ring box from his pocket and dropped to one knee.

Her heart was thudding so hard she couldn't speak. She knew what he was doing, but she hadn't seen this coming and she couldn't believe it was happening now, on a day that was already perfect.

He cracked the leather box open, and she stared at the ring in awe. It was a diamond ring with a huge center stone that sparkled blindingly bright. The center stone was surrounded with smaller diamonds, and tiny diamonds covered the sides of the narrow gleaming band. "It's stunning," she whispered.

"Savannah went shopping with me. I wanted her to tell me what she thought her beloved sister would like best. But she told me that whatever I picked for you would be the one you'd want. And this is the one I picked, because it is like you—beautiful, bright and filled with light." And then he added, his voice pitched even deeper than usual, "Marry me, *agape mou*."

She didn't even have to think about it. "Yes, yes, Nikos, absolutely."

He was on his feet, kissing her, the ring forgotten.

It was much later, after they'd made love and put the ring on her finger and then popped the champagne, that she asked him if they could marry in Greece. "I'd love to have the ceremony at the villa on Kamari, if we could."

"It'd be a very small ceremony, I fear."

"The best kind." She smiled at him and set aside her champagne. She'd had a taste but wouldn't drink more as she was nursing and hated taking chances. "What do you think about just going back...and staying? I want Alek to be raised in Greece. I want him to know his culture. He's not meant to be an American. He's your son—"

"Our son," he corrected.

"Yes, but he's a Panos, and he needs the sun and the sea and lots of space. I do, too."

"You don't have to do this for me, *agapi mou*."

"I know. And I'm doing this for selfish reasons." She struggled to smile, but it was hard with so much emotion filling her. "I want to be with you, and raise our son together, and together we will give him so much love and so much opportunity."

He drew her toward him, kissing her tenderly. "Your love takes my breath away," he said huskily. "You are the sun and the moon and the stars, and every day I thank God for you."

Tears filled her eyes. "You do?"

"I do."

He caressed her cheek, and then kissed her brow, her nose and finally her lips. "Thank you for loving me."

Blinking back tears, she tugged on a strand of his inky-black hair. "I tamed the beast."

"Yes, you did, *yineka mou*. You tamed the beast and turned me into a pussycat."

Georgia laughed. "I wouldn't go that far. You're still not that easy to manage. But it's okay. I'm up for the challenge."

"Good. I love a strong woman." He pressed another kiss to her mouth. "Or maybe it's just you. Because I do love you, and I will love you forever."

* * * * *

*If you enjoyed this Jane Porter story,
look out for her other great reads*

*HIS DEFIANT DESERT QUEEN
THE FALLEN GREEK BRIDE
HIS MAJESTY'S MISTAKE
NOT FIT FOR A KING?
A DARK SICILIAN SECRET*

Available now!

MILLS & BOON®
Hardback – January 2017

ROMANCE

MILLS & BOON®
Large Print – January 2017

ROMANCE

To Blackmail a Di Sione	Rachael Thomas
A Ring for Vincenzo's Heir	Jennie Lucas
Demetriou Demands His Child	Kate Hewitt
Trapped by Vialli's Vows	Chantelle Shaw
The Sheikh's Baby Scandal	Carol Marinelli
Defying the Billionaire's Command	Michelle Conder
The Secret Beneath the Veil	Dani Collins
Stepping into the Prince's World	Marion Lennox
Unveiling the Bridesmaid	Jessica Gilmore
The CEO's Surprise Family	Teresa Carpenter
The Billionaire from Her Past	Leah Ashton

HISTORICAL

Stolen Encounters with the Duchess	Julia Justiss
The Cinderella Governess	Georgie Lee
The Reluctant Viscount	Lara Temple
Taming the Tempestuous Tudor	Juliet Landon
Silk, Swords and Surrender	Jeannie Lin

MEDICAL

Taming Hollywood's Ultimate Playboy	Amalie Berlin
Winning Back His Doctor Bride	Tina Beckett
White Wedding for a Southern Belle	Susan Carlisle
Wedding Date with the Army Doc	Lynne Marshall
Capturing the Single Dad's Heart	Kate Hardy
Doctor, Mummy... Wife?	Dianne Drake

216 GEN STD LP

MILLS & BOON®
Hardback – February 2017

ROMANCE

The Last Di Sione Claims His Prize	Maisey Yates
Bought to Wear the Billionaire's Ring	Cathy Williams
The Desert King's Blackmailed Bride	Lynne Graham
Bride by Royal Decree	Caitlin Crews
The Consequence of His Vengeance	Jennie Lucas
The Sheikh's Secret Son	Maggie Cox
Acquired by Her Greek Boss	Chantelle Shaw
Vows They Can't Escape	Heidi Rice
The Sheikh's Convenient Princess	Liz Fielding
The Unforgettable Spanish Tycoon	Christy McKellen
The Billionaire of Coral Bay	Nikki Logan
Her First-Date Honeymoon	Katrina Cudmore
Their Meant-to-Be Baby	Caroline Anderson
A Mummy for His Baby	Molly Evans
Rafael's One Night Bombshell	Tina Beckett
A Forever Family for the Army Doc	Meredith Webber
The Nurse and the Single Dad	Dianne Drake
The Heir's Unexpected Baby	Jules Bennett
From Enemies to Expecting	Kat Cantrell

MILLS & BOON®
Large Print – February 2017

ROMANCE

The Return of the Di Sione Wife	Caitlin Crews
Baby of His Revenge	Jennie Lucas
The Spaniard's Pregnant Bride	Maisey Yates
A Cinderella for the Greek	Julia James
Married for the Tycoon's Empire	Abby Green
Indebted to Moreno	Kate Walker
A Deal with Alejandro	Maya Blake
A Mistletoe Kiss with the Boss	Susan Meier
A Countess for Christmas	Christy McKellen
Her Festive Baby Bombshell	Jennifer Faye
The Unexpected Holiday Gift	Sophie Pembroke

HISTORICAL

Awakening the Shy Miss	Bronwyn Scott
Governess to the Sheikh	Laura Martin
An Uncommon Duke	Laurie Benson
Mistaken for a Lady	Carol Townend
Kidnapped by the Highland Rogue	Terri Brisbin

MEDICAL

Seduced by the Sheikh Surgeon	Carol Marinelli
Challenging the Doctor Sheikh	Amalie Berlin
The Doctor She Always Dreamed Of	Wendy S. Marcus
The Nurse's Newborn Gift	Wendy S. Marcus
Tempting Nashville's Celebrity Doc	Amy Ruttan
Dr White's Baby Wish	Sue MacKay

MILLS & BOON®

Why shop at millsandboon.co.uk?

Each year, thousands of romance readers find their perfect read at millsandboon.co.uk. That's because we're passionate about bringing you the very best romantic fiction. Here are some of the advantages of shopping at www.millsandboon.co.uk:

* **Get new books first**—you'll be able to buy your favourite books one month before they hit the shops

* **Get exclusive discounts**—you'll also be able to buy our specially created monthly collections, with up to 50% off the RRP

* **Find your favourite authors**—latest news, interviews and new releases for all your favourite authors and series on our website, plus ideas for what to try next

* **Join in**—once you've bought your favourite books, don't forget to register with us to rate, review and join in the discussions

Visit **www.millsandboon.co.uk**
for all this and more today!